Stronger Than Gravity, Faster Than Light

Collective Short Stories

Brought to you by,
Arnab Karmakar

To my parents, Ratna (Ma) & Sudhangshu (Baba)
Karmakar

Author's Note

While this is an anthology of short stories, all these stories are interconnected and reside within the same continuity. The reader may elect to read the stories in any order he/she pleases, but may appreciate them better when all stories are read in order.

Also, any names or similarities to actual people remain purely coincidental.

The companion website to this anthology can be found
at http://www.arnabkarmakar.net
You may follow the author on twitter: @karmakar

Index

A Wedding Invitation

Finally! Danny recognized it exactly when he looked into his mailbox and saw the colorful envelope resting on top of the stack of Wednesday mail. After being engaged for a year and a half, his best friend Sunil was getting married in the upcoming July. Since Sunil was marrying his college sweetheart, Justine, of Polish and Lithuanian heritage, and Catholic, two disparate ceremonies were scheduled. The Hindu ceremony was to occur on a Friday night with the Catholic one following promptly the next morning. Sunil naturally asked Danny to be the best man at the Catholic ceremony.

Sorting the mail, he tucked the bundle under his arm while he grabbed the house key out of the right pocket of his khaki slacks. At age of twenty-five and three years out of college, Danny still lived with his parents. It didn't bother him, just as it didn't during the four years of college when he had elected to commute to Rutgers. His parents gave him the option of choosing between life in the dormitory or a new car. It did not take long to decide that a red-hot Celica felt more attractive than the food that the Rutgers dining halls had to offer.

He originally didn't intend to go to college so close to home. But after a shoulder injury made it improbable that he would be wrestling for Lehigh or Indiana, he found Rutgers to be the best option for him. Unlike some of the small four-year colleges that still showed an interest in him, it had affordable tuition.

Attending Rutgers marked the first time since fifth grade when he would not have a class with Sunil. Sunil got in early decision to Columbia, where he shortly toyed with pre-medical studies before switching over to his passion in computer science. Besides being a consistent Dean's List student, Sunil played on the lacrosse team and kept a steady relationship during his last three years. Every summer, he got an internship at either a financial or a consulting firm in New York City, while Danny usually worked at the mall or at a lab, and his grandfather would constantly pester him to be like his friend and pursue more glamorous jobs.

Danny walked into an empty house. His father, a high school gym teacher, was probably coaching a team of junior high school wrestlers, and today, it was his mother's turn to serve the late shift at the library. Had it been five years ago, his golden retriever, Hulk, would have rushed to greet him. After his death, he did not care to get another dog. A cherished memory of his dog rested in a framed picture that hung right above the entrance to the family room. Glancing at the picture, he thought that his dog could have been a show dog. Danny was in the picture too, kneeling, his arm around his dog. It must have been taken in junior high, since in it his left ear didn't have the small looped earring he always wore. Since in the picture Danny wore his favorite Yankees baseball cap, looking at it, no one would be able to tell he had red hair, which was a legacy of his great grandfather, whose name he also bore. Legend had it that in the Mahoney family, every four generations would be born a red head. Danny knew no other redheads in his family.

Ripping the envelope open with his fingers, Danny slouched on the family room couch, turning on the television to ESPN. He laughed at the cover of the card. The brown groom wore a tuxedo and the white bride donned a sari. The couple stood on top of the globe, holding hands. The top of the card said "Joining Faith". He wondered if it was a typo, if it meant to say "Joining in Faith", but decided not to give it much more thought. Justine's father, who owned a printing press, probably designed it.

Danny found it a bit peculiar that he would be sent an invitation, even if it was just part of the formality. Justine's parents could have saved themselves at least fifty cents in postage. Maybe they

7

had heard of his grandfather's reputation and felt that the card may shed some light on his parochial ways. Whatever! He grabbed a pen off the coffee table, and on the RSVP card, marked two, for the number of attendees. He carefully wrote Danny Mahoney and Rina Desai, and sealed it.

The card made him think about Sunil, and he decided to call him. No one answered, and a message resembling Justine's voice greeted. Danny disconnected, deciding not to leave a message. Both of them were still probably at work. Sunil worked at a management consulting firm, and he was probably still at the client site. At least twice a week, he traveled to Chicago for a data-warehousing project. Justine worked in the same Wall Street firm in which Rina did, though she would resign soon so that she could return to Columbia to pursue her MBA.

Less than two years of work experience, and she was already pursuing an MBA. Undoubtedly when his grandfather would hear of this, he would badger Danny as to why he could not find a girl like the one Sunil had found. According to the old man, it would make more sense for Sunil to be dating Rina. After three years of countless arguments, Danny now found it futile to tell his grandfather that even though Sunil and Rina both came from India, their cultures bore little to no similarities. They did not even speak the same language.

Perhaps he would ask his parents to bring along the old man to the wedding. It would be a good way to prep the old geezer for what in a year or two, would be the greatest shock of his life: that children borne of a brown woman would carry on his family name.

Danny already began to mull about the speech he would recite at the reception. He would say how much he admired and respected Sunil. Even if Sunil was his age, in certain respects, Danny considered him a role model. He would begin to emulate him, so that he too could live a life of happiness. Rina would be in for a pleasant surprise.

Had it not been for Sunil's family, he would be unable to break the ice with Rina as quickly and successfully as he had done. It had gone so smoothly and spontaneously, and though it happened three years ago during his last semester of college, the vivid memory felt like it could have happened yesterday. At around eleven on a Monday morning in the computer science building, he went to office hours for the algorithms class he was taking. She walked into the office where he was already having exponential growth explained to him by his professor, a Brazilian who had a heavy accent, but nonetheless, spoke good English.

"Hi," she interrupted the conversation without being rude. No doubt she was an Indian. There could be no possibility of confusing her for a Latina or even a Pakistani. He had seen her several times before from a distance, either at the student center studying, or at the gym, where she would spend her time on the stair master. He never bothered to approach her, but he would stare at her for several moments. She had an undeniably pretty face, which commanded respect and awe. He would wonder if she were a snob, but then thought that she probably didn't reveal herself as easily. Observing her composure, standing straight up and confident, her Whitemountain backpack clinging to her with only one strap, he knew her upbringing would have definitely been in the states. He could detect only the slightest hint of an accent in her tone. "Do you have an extra book?"

"I'm sorry?" said the professor.

"The algorithms book. The bookstore sold out and won't get the next shipment until Friday. I was wondering if you had an extra book you could lend out until then?"

The professor shook his head. "Sorry, this is my only copy. You can photocopy the first two chapters if you like."

"Oh," she said. "Okay."

Seeing an opportunity he did not want to blow away, Danny promptly zipped up his backpack and waved his own book in the air. "I'll make the copies for you."

"Oh, thanks." Her perpetual smile broadened, and he was able to see his own reflection in her beautiful brown eyes.

He walked with her to the math postal office, via the bridge that annexed the math and computer science headquarters. Staring outside the fiberglass windows, he saw that the snow on the ground remained intact despite the bright sun, making its appearance go unnoticeable. Danny noticed a certain class to her. Neither short, nor too tall, she stood a head shorter than him. Her perpetual smile bewitched him, and she did have good taste in clothes: a bright Nautica jacket, black Calvin Klein jeans, which were not skin tight. He did not care to look at her shoes, but instead, stared at his own sneakers, and then rushed ahead to open the door for her.

She smiled to say thank you. "So, how much am I going to owe you?"

"What's that?"

"The copies. How much am I going to owe you for them?"

"Oh, don't worry about it!"

"No, I can't let you pay for all those copies."

"Who said anything about paying?"

"You're getting them for free?"

"Yep! I used to work at the math library," he explained. "If you do like anything for the math department, they let you get unlimited use of their copy machine. No one ever bothered to deactivate my user name."

"Oh wow." They kept on walking. He could feel that he was failing to impress her.

"Well, it's not really unlimited," he added on. "We got a limit of nine hundred ninety nine thousand nine hundred and ninety nine. I'm surprised I didn't surpass it already." He managed to get a laugh out of

10

her. "Seriously, this machine like saved me like a mint each semester with all the copies I had to do."

"By the way," she said. "I'm Rina."

Bingo. Sunil had an aunt named Rina. This probably meant she was from Bengal, either the Kolkata area or Bangladesh. Now that he had established common ground, he could start work. He extended his hand to her. "Rina! That's a really nice name."

"What about you?" She stared at him, as if he had forgotten the obvious.

"What about me?" He said that as timidly and defensively as he could.

"Do you have a name?"

"Oh, my fault. Danny! Danny Mahoney."

"Nice to meet you."

There were already two people ahead of them to use the copy machine, but it did not bother him. "So, what part of India are you from? Bengal?"

She looked at him, surprised. "No. I'm not Bengali. I'm Marathi. It's . . ."

"You mean the Bombay area?"

"Yeah!"

"So I guess you celebrate Diwali and Holi?"

"Yeah. How do you know so much?"

"Can't you tell," he smiled triumphantly. "I'm Indian."

"No, really," she laughed. "How do you know?"

He told her how since the fifth grade, he had a best friend named Sunil Sarkar, who lived down the street from him. Sunil's older sister got married a while back to a Punjabi guy whose family had settled in the Bombay area. He went on to add that Sunil's parents were very cultured, and they would often conduct ceremonies at home such as the Narayan Puja or the Lakshmi Puja. He would always be invited. Even when the Bengali community would hold some festivals such as the Durga Puja, and rent places like Scott Hall at the main campus of Rutgers, Danny would accompany the Sarkar family. The first time he went to a Puja, he did

11

nothing more than walk around the campus of Scott Hall with Sunil, and eventually joined in a touch football game with the other Bengali kids there.

She asked him what he thought about the Pujas. He admitted that when he first went to one in fifth grade, he did not understand the essence of it. For a religious ceremony, it seemed to be quite loud, and there was a lot of socialization occurring. And the Goddess Durga, who people worshipped, seemed a bit bellicose with her ten arms, most carrying a lethal weapon. To him, it looked like a villain taken out of a fantasy game. But Mr. Sarkar explained to him that this was a symbol of God attacking evil with a vengeance, so it all made sense. "But when I went to another Puja like a couple weeks later," he went on, " I started to feel like a little guilty.

"Why?"

"Because, you know like I'm Catholic and all, and we're not supposed to worship more than one God. . . . ."

"So?"

"So, at one Puja they were worshipping the Goddess Durga, and at the one they had two or three weeks later, they were worshipping the Goddess Kali. I felt like I was breaking the first commandment. But then I talked to Sunil's mom and she assured me that these two Goddesses were really the same. It was like God does many different things for us and we use a different day to thank Him for a different deed."

By the time he completed his dialogue, he had also finished making the photocopies for her. She listened to him with complacent curiosity. "Wow, you know a lot about Hinduism."

He shrugged, handing her the copies. "I guess it's one of my hobbies. You know, reading up on other religions and all."

"Is religion your minor?"

"Nope, comp.sci."

"Really? But I thought that was your major?"

"Nope. But I'm beginning to wish it was. Then I probably wouldn't be heading for the unemployment office straight out of graduation."

"Why, what's your major?"

"Bio-chem!"

"Really?" she smiled. "That's what I was going to major in freshman year. But I switched over to computer science and economics."

"That's a good combo," he nodded his head. "I wish I was smart enough to do something like that. You looking for work?"

"Not anymore. I have a couple of offers from some Wall Street firms."

"Cool! I wish I was in your shoes."

"Why, what kind of work are you looking for? The bio-chem should say something about your quantitative skills. Maybe you could try to find some work as a financial analyst!"

"At this point, I'll take anything that'll get me a decent paycheck!"

"Aren't you thinking about med school at all?"

"Yeah right. Maybe I thought about it for like five minutes freshman year" he laughed, at himself. "But with my GPA, the only schools that'd take me are the Carribeans."

"You never know. Did you even take the MCATs?"

"Nah, I was never really interested in doing medicine. I don't even know why I majored in science. I always liked math better."

"Didn't you ever think about changing your major?"

"Yeah, but by the time I thought about it, I was already a junior, and I'd have to stay in school longer than I want. Anyway, I was too far into my major to just quit. Like, you remember how much of a joke intro to chem was, right?"

She shook her head. "I had AP credit for that. For me, it was orgo, and that was it!"

"Yeah, I had credit for bio, but I didn't bother taking the AP chem exam. If I took organic my first year, it probably would hit me then and there how much I hated it. Even if I took bio in college, it probably would've occurred to me to try something else. The only thing I can do with my degree is like flip burgers."

"No, don't say that. I'm sure you'll find something," she assured him. "You look like a bright guy."

And so they became study partners. At least once a week they would get together to study computer algorithms, which would result in their going out to lunch or dinner together at the Busch student center. Since she was a vegetarian, he would either order a pizza or a salad to accommodate her. He would tell her many things. He told her that he was a diehard Yankees fan, Giants fan, and a Knick fan, though in high school, he only wrestled. He would have played baseball too had he gotten along with the coach, who once caught Danny and his friends smoking marijuana near school grounds. Sunil and the others managed to run away without being identified, but the coach somehow recognized Danny. The next morning, he demanded to know the names of the other culprits. Danny refused, and the coach agreed that it would be best if they severed all relations with each other.

She asked why he chose not to wrestle for Rutgers, and he told her that he was no longer good enough to compete at a division one school. He would only participate in intramurals. "You said you wrestled varsity for three years," she asked him. "Did any school want you?"

He explained that a couple of small liberal arts schools in Pennsylvania made some noise, but none of them were much of academic institutions. Rutgers made more sense. He asked why she chose Rutgers, and she told him that Rutgers offered a lot more financial aid than Barnard.

He liked that he had to ask questions to learn more about her. Had he not asked he would not have known that she lived in Woodbridge, a town not far from Rutgers. She did not commute because both her parents worked, and had only two cars. Her father, a trained chemical engineer, worked at a startup-consulting firm, which consisted mostly of Indians. He worked at a client site fifty miles away. Her mother worked for a travel agency in Rahway, not far at all from her house. She had an older sister who got married a year and a half ago, and lived in Philadelphia with her husband, a doctor doing his residency in dermatology. Curious as to why her sister had an arranged marriage, he asked her, "Was your sister born in India?"

"Yeah," she sounded surprised that he missed the obvious. "So was I."

"Really, I didn't know that? When'd you come here? When you were really little, right?"

"No! When I came here, I was going into eleventh grade."

That he did not expect. Doing the math in his head, he realized that if her sister graduated three years ago, she should be around twenty-five. Give or take a year. He needed to move more quickly. "I would have never guessed it," he told her with utmost seriousness. He found it incredible that she did not speak with a heavy accent.

It really would not bother him had she had an accent. Not as much as it would have if she had a boyfriend. She probably didn't, if her family still practiced arranged marriages. Out of all the months he had been talking to her, she had never mentioned a boyfriend, which probably meant she was single. But if there was one social lesson he learned from his junior year of college, it was not to make assumptions, regardless of what first met the eye. He had been okay; he could wrestle. Violence, however, didn't suit him, and he did not enjoy stigmatizing his fellow man. But he did need to move fast.

He had a plan and a deadline, yet he paced himself. "Are you going to live at home when you start working?" he asked her, one day, while they were studying for the algorithms midterm at the math library.

"Probably forever," she slouched against her chair, letting her mechanical pencil fall into the middle of her open book. She turned her head towards him, smiling, as if to say thank you, for giving her an excuse to take a break.

"C'mon now. You're not going to live with your parents forever."

"Yes! Forever! Hopefully."

"But by forever, you don't mean forever, right?" he kept his fingers crossed underneath the table. "You probably mean just for like a couple of years, so you can save up some money, right? I mean, you don't want to be living with them when you're married and got kids . . ."

She laughed so hard that an older woman sitting on the other side of the bookcase walked over and asked them to keep it down. He apologized on their behalf. "You found that funny?" he asked, feeling a bit disturbed.

"Well, yeah! You're asking me about things so far down the road. Right now, I'm just worried about graduating and moving back home."

"Yeah, but you've got to dream too. You know, like exponential growth. What matters most is how the function behaves as things go to infinity." He had been waiting all semester to use that line, but regretted that he could not make it sound as romantic as intended. She stared at him perplexed, and all of a sudden, he felt like a geek who tried to impress the girl by being a pedant. "Like you've got to see what's best for you in the long run."

"I know what you were trying to say. It was just cute the way you tried to phrase it," she reassured him. "Yeah, I see what you're saying, but don't you have to worry about the present first so that you can shape the future?"

"True, you've got a point. But to build the present, shouldn't you use your idea of the future as a model?"

Instead of answering, she said, "What about you? Do you have your entire future planned out?"

"I did!"

"What do you mean you did?" Suddenly her voice sounded concerned. "What happened?"

"Things just didn't work out with me and Lynne."

Her smile began to fade. "You mean your ex-girlfriend?"

"Uh huh. Man, am I glad she's out of my life. It's like I had everything planned out with her. I'd like propose to her, and I figured out where we'd be living, and how many kids we'd have . . ."

"What," she chuckled. "Did you actually tell her this?"

"No, I'm not crazy. I kept all that to myself. I only went out with her for like a couple of months."

"And you had all this planned out already?"

"Well, yes and no. I knew eventually I wanted to start a family. Just not with her. Definitely not with her."

"You're saying that now because she broke up with you," she reminded him.

"No, I'm saying that because she's a fucking idiot. I don't think I ever had like a decent conversation with her that even came close to being labeled as intelligent."

"If you were so unhappy with her, why did you stay with her for so long?"

Danny shrugged his shoulders, stared up at the ceiling, and popped his bubble gum. He stared at her pretty face. Her hair was pulled back, but thin pieces were hanging across her face. "Beats me. I guess I just wanted to be happy. I mean, here I saw Sunil and

Justine all really happy together. They even got a place together that they're moving into in June."

"Really?" She said it so loud, that the woman came back, this time accompanied by a librarian, a fifth year engineering student who Danny knew when he worked here. He had also seen him back in high school when he would attend wrestling tournaments. The librarian acknowledged him, but told him that if they felt the need to talk, they should probably find a better place to study. Danny and Rina both packed their bags, since they decided that they had done enough studying for the night. Danny apologized for any disturbance he may have created.

On the way out, he held the door for her, but she lightly pushed him to go first. "Sunil and Justine are really moving in together?"

"Yep. They found a one bedroom in the Upper East Side."

"And their parents are okay with this?"

"I don't know about Justine's parents, but I was kind of surprised to see that Sunil's parents were okay with it. I doubt that my parents would be so cool if I did something like that."

She breathed a sigh of relief.

"No, but Sunil's been really happy since he's known Justine. I guess I kind of thought if I got a blonde too, I'd be just as happy. Lynne's hair was like as blonde as mine is red."

"Well, I'm sure you'll have other blondes in your life."

"God, I hope not." Inadvertently, he pulled out his wallet, and searched for a picture hidden beneath a bundle of business cards. He was about to throw it into the trashcan, when Rina asked him what he was looking at. As if against his willpower, he handed it to her. "It's Lynne."

Rina perused the picture. She saw a fair girl with golden hair and beautiful blue eyes. Her sleeveless black dress exposed a conspicuous part of her cleavage,

18

and flaunted her enviable figure. Rina handed the picture back to Danny. "She's very pretty. If you want to be happy, you should lower your standards."

Being stuck inside the library all day studying, they missed the pleasant day. Now with nightfall, came a chilly wind. Danny could feel his blue tear away pants flapping against his knees and shins. He would have taken off his jacket and wrapped it around her, but she was already wearing her Nautica coat. Fortunately, he had parked his car in the parking lot right outside her dorm, so he had an excuse to walk her back. She talked about the exam, how they were ready for it, but he really could not listen. He still had Lynne's picture in his hand. An abrupt dose of anger was tormenting his mind. What did she mean by lowering his standards? He had already told her that Lynne's beauty was only skin deep. How superficial did she think he was? He could feel the color of his hair diffusing across his face, acutely in his ears. The anger shielded him from the penetrating wind.

" . . . And I think we're ready . . ." Mulling about her comment, he failed to realize that they walked right outside of her dorm.

"Well, thanks for all your help," she said to him. "Goodnight!"

He did not respond, but watched her graciously walk towards the entrance. She opened her bag, and searched for her key card. That instant she got the door open, he screamed angrily. "Rina!"

She promptly turned, and when she saw him, she became abruptly concerned. Walking quickly towards him, she said, "What happened? Are you alright?"

"I'm not going to do it!" he shouted at her.

"What?"

"Do what you said about Lynne," he yelled at her with the new found intensity with which one finally confronts a bully. "There's no way in hell I'm going to lower my standards. You got that?"

She crouched in fear after each word he uttered, as if to dodge physical assault. She did not have the

19

courage to run away, afraid that he would leap on her like a tiger. "Oh," she avoided eye contact, and stared in the direction of the parked cars. "Sorry, I was just . . ."

"I just raised them," he interrupted her gently. Dropping his knapsack against the gravel of the sidewalk, he placed his hands on either side of her frost bitten cheeks. If he did not know better, he would have said that the minuscule tears at the corners of her eyes were a result of the cruel winds. Bringing his lips over hers', he lost his fingers in her silky black hair. The picture of Lynne escaped from his hand and flew with the wind into oblivion.

The instant he saw a white Honda pull out, Danny turned on his blinker. Even on a late afternoon at the beginning of the week, the parking lot to Bridgewater Commons mall was always full. Finally he found a spot near the entrance, but still far enough for him to enjoy a good walk. He waved at the Indian lady driving the Honda, who did not care to return the gesture. Maybe it could have been Rina's mother. If it were, he would not be able to recognize her, because the last time he had seen her was a couple of years ago. He doubted that it was she. If she had the need to go shopping, she would most likely go to the mall right by her house.

Getting out of his red Celica, he jogged to the side entrance, pulling up the zipper on his fleece. Like usual, he had underestimated the weather of early March. What he really needed were gloves, and to compensate for that, he dug his hands into the pockets of his jacket, which took him a while to find. The various people who walked in and out of the mall were prepared to face the weather, armed with wool coats and hats.

The mall quickly helped him forget about the chilly weather. Climbing down the escalator, he saw a couple of kids who could not have been more than sophomores in high school, hanging out outside a software store, probably talking about how cool the latest strategy game was. All of them wore baggy pants at least two sizes too large. He wondered if he ever looked that stupid back in high school. Next as he descended onto the ground floor, Danny saw a young Asian couple, either Korean or Filipino walk past him. They seemed happily in love. The guy had his arm around his girlfriend, whose head rested on his shoulder. Danny watched them, as they got smaller and smaller and eventually disappeared, turning into a store that sold luggage. Maybe they were planning their honeymoon.

Danny walked into the jewelry shop that had two attendees behind the counters. He saw no other customers there. Staring at the prices, Danny understood why.

"Can I help you?" the slightly overweight bearded man, with a baldhead approached him. The man seemed in his fifties. Yet, he had a young man's voice, and if you talked to him on the phone, you would think that he was in college. Danny searched the man's navy blue shirt for a nametag, could only see that colorful tie, and a pen in the shirt pocket.

"Maybe she could," he pointed towards the other salesperson, a tall thin woman, with long brown hair. She looked like she could have been either in her early thirties, or late twenties. "I need to know what a gorgeous lady would like for her three year anniversary."

"Sure!" The bald man interceded. "I can help you with that. Follow me." He walked behind a counter at the far end of the store. "So, how much are you looking to spend?"

"Honestly, I haven't the slightest idea. I'm just looking for something that'll say 'I love you'." Seeing the man's greedy eyes, he added, "Maybe like two hundred dollars. At most."

The bald man opened the case behind him and pulled out a gold necklace. "How about this? It's a bargain. Only a hundred and forty dollars!"

Danny shook his head. Rina already had a twenty-two karat gold necklace she usually wore. "I was hoping for something more like a ring or a bracelet. Maybe silver."

"How about this," the bald man pulled out a thin silver oval ring, which sported a small shiny diamond. His late grandmother had worn something quite similar.

"I'll tell you what. Why don't I think about it! I'll get back to you in a couple of weeks."

"Can't promise you that it'll still be here."

"I'll take my chances," Danny turned his head, smiling on the way out.

The drive back home took longer than he anticipated. It would have been much more convenient for him to go to Menlo Park Mall, which from his house, was a two-minute drive, a twelve-minute walk. But then he ran the risk of running into one of Rina's friends, maybe Rina herself. Even if Rina did work in New York City, it would be just his luck that she should decide to take a half-day, and come back home to shop.

He pulled his car up to the driveway and sighed when he saw the Grand Cherokee in his driveway. His parents could have warned him that his grandfather would be stopping by.

Danny slowly got out of his car, and walked over to the mailbox, watching every small step he took. He checked the empty mailbox, and walked on the outer perimeter of the driveway. Reaching the front door, he pulled out his key, in spite of his parents' tendency to leave it unlocked when they were home.

"Danny boy how are ya?" His grandfather sat in the armchair in the living room, talking to his dad. His grandfather's silver hair was perfectly parted, and judging by his tie, and perfectly ironed white shirt, one would think that the man had just come home from work. But had had been retired from the narcotics department of the police force for over a decade.

"Hey Gramps," he tried to sound as apathetic as possible.

"Danny," his mother walked in wearing an apron and an oven mitten. Her shoulder length brown hair was pulled back into a bun. "Where were you? Your father already ate."

"I told you I was going to stop by the mall."

"Well, wash up. We're waiting for you, Honey"

Danny gladly kicked off his shoes and walked into the kitchen, towards the sink.

"Later Dan," he heard his father call out. "I promised to help with Little League tryouts."

"Did you say hello to your grandfather?" his mother said when she walked into the kitchen.

"Yes Mom!" He took a seat at the glass oval kitchen table. The table was already set. His mother had cooked pasta and grilled chicken. While they said grace, Danny peeked open his eye and looked at his grandfather. The man's eyes were tightly shut, and he passionately chanted his prayer. When he crossed himself, he looked like he was trying to show off. Danny stared at the ring on his right hand. After they said Amen and began to load their plates, Danny thought about the jewelry shop. "Hey Gramps . . . "

The phone rang, and Danny impulsively volunteered to get it. It was for him, but it was just a tele-marketer, trying to sell him a subscription to the *Reader's Digest*. He said he was not interested, and hung up.

"So, how's your friend doing?" His grandfather asked as he sat back down.

"She's not my friend. She's my . . ."

"Danny, honey," his mother interceded. "I think your grandfather is talking about Sunil."

He turned to his grandfather, who nodded his head while he chewed on his white meat. "Oh! He's doing alright."

"I'd say he's doing more than just alright!"

"Sure, I guess. If you say so."

"How's he liking work? Where does he work again? AT&T?"

"Andersen!" He had lost count how many times had answered this question for the old man. It wasn't like the two companies were even in similar industries.

"That's a great company," his grandfather pointed his fork in his direction, as if he was a professor giving a lecture.

"It's okay."

"Just okay? He must be making big bucks over there."

"I really wouldn't know." This was a lie. Even in their mid-twenties, Danny and Sunil were in the habit of telling each other everything. "We have better things to talk about than how much we make."

"Well, I'm sure he must be making at least a small fortune. Getting a place in the city isn't as cheap as living at home. Maybe you should send him your resume. See if he can set you up with something."

"I've got a job," he reminded the old man. "I like where I am. It's only a few minutes from home, and I'm learning lots. Anyway, I really don't want to do consulting."

It had taken him a while, but a few months after graduating college, Danny joined a software startup that was launched by a Rutgers Graduate student who was doing his Ph.D. in computer science.

"How would you know if you never tried it?"

Danny felt like yelling at the man, telling him to shut up. Try something new? The man was so far to the right, his idea of trying something new was to read the same laws from a different book. "I do try new things. I'm just not so psyched about doing consulting. Okay?"

"Danny, there's no need to lose your temper," he had practically forgotten about his mother's presence. She would keep going back and forth from the table to the stovetop. Twice, she went to answer the phone.

Staring at his grandfather vindictively, he ripped apart a roll of bread. "It's Sunil's girl who brings in the big bucks. That's how he can afford that place he's got."

"Living off his woman, is he?"

"Yeah," Danny laughed. "Times are changing. Pretty soon, before we know it, being a housewife might become a man's everyday job."

"I wouldn't go that far."

"Relax Gramps. It was only a joke."

"Well, you're not the only one who can have a sense of humor," his grandfather smiled affectionately.

"No, but really, Sunil couldn't have found a better girl for himself. She's everything he's ever wanted in a soul mate."

"Soul mate? So, they're really serious about the relationship?"

"I guess. They're getting married in a few months."

"Is that so?"

Danny glanced at this mother who quickly and politely shook her head. At least twice before, his grandfather had been informed of Sunil's engagement. He was even invited to attend the engagement party, but had declined to go. He said he had some old friends visiting that day.

"Yeah."

"Well, I'll say my prayers for him. I really hope things work out for him."

Danny wiped his face with his napkin. Crumpling it up into a ball, he tossed it onto his plate. "Why wouldn't it?"

"Wouldn't what?"

"Things work out for him? He's been dating the girl for like since college. I think they know each other by now!"

"But what about when they have kids?" The old man felt like he had a point and driven someone up against a wall.

"What about them?" Danny had exhausted all his patience. Silently, he vowed this would be the last decent thing he would say to the old man today.

"What faith will they have? How will they raise them?"

"Any damn way they please!"

"Danny," he heard his mother's admonishment.

"No, no, it's okay Erin," the old man soothed his daughter-in-law. His face had maintained its calm composure. "I see that young Danny here's got a lot to learn!"

Danny rose to his feet so violently that his chair slid back and slammed against the end of the kitchen counter. A cardboard box of salt that was resting on the edge of the counter-top, fell on top the brownish marble tiles, covering a large portion of it white. "You know something, I think you're the reason they say that you can't teach an old dog new tricks. Why the hell do you have to be so damn stubborn all the time?"

"Danny," the old man said, calmly but didactically. "Clean it up!"

"Give me an answer damn it."

"I have conservative tastes."

"Oh no," he walked over towards the cabinet where the dustpan was. Sweeping up the salt, he said, "Don't hide behind all that conservative bull crap. I don't mind conservative. I like being conservative. But you're no conservative. You're just plain as hell stubborn!" After throwing away the salt in the garbage, he replaced the dustpan. "How they raise their kids is their business. Maybe they'll raise them Catholic, maybe they'll raise them Hindu, maybe they'll raise them as both. Either way, it's none of your business. You got that?"

"Daniel," his mother got out of her chair, and cautiously approached him. "Please calm down. You're upset. You're saying things that . . ."

Inadvertently he shoved away the arm she put around him. "I mean exactly what I'm saying. I'm sick of always giving in just so I have to accommodate this guy."

Rather than being offended, the old man simply laughed at Danny. "How can you raise a child in two faiths?"

26

He glared at the old man. After wrecking a pleasant evening and engineering an unnecessary fight, he still wore the same composure. There was not a hint of melancholy in him that the normal person would feel after being disgraced by his grandson. "Like I said," he walked out into the corridor where his fleece and shoes were dutifully waiting for him. He now had his back towards the old man. "You can't teach an old dog new tricks!"

As he stepped outside, his mother called out asking where he was going. "Out!" he cried, letting the door slam shut behind him. He would definitely say the jewelry shop deserved another visit later on during the week.

"Thanks for coming out here in such short notice." There was still a hint of daylight out there. When they walked past the tennis courts and heard that incessant bouncing of the yellow ball, he noticed that the lights had yet to be turned on. The ranger must've just mowed the lawn, since the green grass still looked as fresh as his recently cut hair. And he could hear the fading sound of the motor some distance away.

"Oh. It's no trouble at all," Rina squeezed his fingers with hers'. She was wearing khaki ladies' pants and a blue button down which she did not bother to tuck in or button all the way. Many years ago, that shirt used to be his. In spite of the weather, he had never seen her wear shorts. Either slacks, or knee length skirts, but never shorts. He on the other hand, would wear shorts every chance possible. He probably owned more pairs of shorts than he did slacks. He probably even owned more baseball caps than he did slacks. "Anyway, I'm getting used to it by now."

"Hah, hah, very funny!" A man riding his mountain bike zoomed past them, clothed in bright spandex, and a plastic helmet. Danny looked over his shoulder to watch the biker gradually disappear behind the scenery of green trees and bushes. He thought it to

27

be really awkward that a man so old would require a helmet. He might as well have training wheels on too.

"... Why do you let him bother you so much?"

"Huh? I'm sorry? What?"

"Your grandfather! Why do you let him get to you so much?"

"I told you the things that son of a bitch says to me."

"Danny, that's so mean," her face became greatly disturbed. "You shouldn't talk about your elders like that!"

"He obviously doesn't give a shit about me. So why should I give two shits about him?"

"He does care about you!" They ceased walking when she let go of his hand. She positioned herself directly in front of him, and started to play with his Hawaiian beaded necklace. "He's your grandfather. He loves you."

"Well, he has a funny way of showing it. It's always like Sunil this and Sunil that, and Sunil's got a great job and it's like he's trying to make me out to be some sort of a fucking loser."

"Danny, you're not a loser."

"I know I'm not. I'm happy with my life."

"Then why are you letting someone else put you down? Especially someone who's growing older day after day!"

Danny failed to gather the courage to tell her that his grandfather had strong quandaries about the success of Sunil's marriage. How could he tell her that the man whose lineage she would help continue did not believe in the concept of East meeting West? "I don't know why you're defending the man. I mean, you remember how he treated you whenever he saw you?"

"He wasn't mean to me," she countered him gently.

"Wasn't what you'd call nice either!"

"You want to know something," he noticed his reflection in her beautiful brown eyes. "I don't care how other people treat me as long as I know that you're going to stand up for me."

"Then you've got nothing to worry about!" He bent down to give her a kiss. Disgruntled chuckles interrupted him. Turning his head, he saw three kids, probably elementary school age, staring at his direction. All of them looked Indian. One was riding a razor scooter, and the other two were on bikes. The instant they noticed him staring at their direction, they fled away in the direction of the basketball courts.

Taking Rina by the hand, he led her to a bench that faced the softball field. He rested against the stone arm of the bench, and she rested herself against his torso, her head against his shoulder. Taking his arm, she wrapped it around herself like a blanket. "Thanks," he whispered into her ear.

"For what?"

"For being you!"

"Oh," he could hear her laugh, feel her smile. "No need to thank me." He kissed the top of her silky black hair. The softball field brought back old memories of Little League. His Dad, the coach, would often conduct practices here at least twice a week. His team won the World Series twice. The best player on the team was a kid named Lonnie Friedman, who played first base, and batted cleanup. Lonnie had a black father and a white mother. Quite the versatile athlete, Lonnie excelled at football, basketball, and baseball. In high school, besides being known for his athletic feats, he had also developed a reputation for being a bit of a trouble maker, since he would often cut class and spend time in in-school suspension. Overall, though, Danny felt that Lonnie was a nice kid, and had he been given the proper guidance, he perhaps would have made a name for himself at some division one school.

He leaned over to get a glance of Rina's face, which stared at the darkening sky. "What are you thinking about?"

"Oh, nothing."

"Don't say nothing," he tickled her. "You're thinking about something. What is it?"

"Just about the wedding."

He hugged her tighter, like she was his favorite stuffed animal. The last time he had one of those he was seven. "What about it?"

"I can't wait for it. I've never been to one where they have two ceremonies."

"Yeah, it should be a good experience!"

"What?"

"It should be lots of fun."

"Oh, yeah. Have you ever been to one of those before?"

"Sure. Freshman year, when Sunil's sister got married."

"Yeah, but that was to a Punjabi guy. I'm talking about a marriage where a Christian married a Hindu."

"Oh, no. This one'll be my first."

"It'll be my first too," her tone sounded sensual. It occurred to him, that out of the three years they had been dating, it had taken a year to take her to bed with him. He was in no rush for it, and the wait was well worth it. He felt like Doogie Howser, in that while he had slept with other girls in the past, with Rina he made love for the first time. His first time had been with a girl was in high school, during prom weekend. The girl was from his town, but she went to a different school, a private school. He dated her for four months, asked her to his prom, and then shared with her a night of passion. Shortly afterwards, she broke up with him. Since she was going to college out west, she did not feel like being in a long distance relationship. He tried to keep in touch thereafter, but after his freshman year of college, he lost all trace of her. The one thing he remembered vividly about her was her blonde hair.

"There's a first time for everything," he kissed the top of Rina's silky black hair.

"So, what're you getting them?"

Danny shrugged. "Don't know. Haven't gotten them anything yet!"

"What're you waiting for? You've had almost a year to get them something."

"Relax, it's not like they're getting married tomorrow."

"Yeah, but don't you have an idea of what you want to get them?"

"Actually," he shook his head. " I was kind of hoping you'd give me one."

"Me? How?"

"Well, since we're going together, maybe we should get them something together."

"Oh, okay," she pivoted her body so that she was facing him. "We can do that."

"Cool, then it's a date," he softly kissed the top of her forehead.

He had never seen her without jewelry. She would always be wearing earrings and quite often, she would sport that gold necklace that carried a locket of Lord Krishna. Taking her hands in his, he realized that each of her ten fingers was completely naked.
His grandfather was right about one thing. The time was coming for him to move out.

When they finally agreed on a day, which they could dedicate solely to shopping, they encountered another obstacle. Where would they go shopping?
"What's wrong with Bridgewater?" He asked her on the phone. He sat on his bed, tying his sneakers. He heard on the radio that it was supposed to be a nice day, so naturally he dressed in shorts, and a long sleeved white T-shirt.

"It's so far away!"

"What are you talking about far away? It's only like fifteen minutes. Tops!"

"Yeah, but why waste all that extra gas?"

"I don't care. It's only like a ninety-nine-cent difference. If even! What do you care? I'm the one that's driving."

"Come on Danny," she whined. "I like Menlo better."

"Why? Bridgewater's like twice as big and's got like four times as many stores."

"But Menlo has everything we need. Please Danny. Please."

"Alright, alright, fine. I'll pick you up in like fifteen minutes."

He did not know why he even let that meager argument grow. She was right. Menlo would be a much more convenient trip for him. He had been spending so much time at Bridgewater lately, that it had become somewhat like his favorite sweatshirt, which he would find every excuse to wear, but had not worn out quite yet.

He found her waiting promptly at the corner of her block. At first he thought she was wearing shorts, but it turned out to be a silk skirt. Her arms were crossed around her white short-sleeved cotton sweater, and her brown Ray Ban sunglasses were protecting her eyes from the sun. Her house, a brown ranch, was located much further down the street. He had seen it several times when dropping her off home at night. He only saw the interior when she would show him photographs.

"If we don't find anything at Menlo, we're heading straight to Bridgewater. Deal?"

"What's your obsession with Bridgewater?" she kissed his cheek hello. His CD player blasted a Beastie Boys' album, but she turned on the radio and adjusted it to a station that specialized in light songs.

It took them at least ten minutes to find a space on the outer perimeters of the Menlo parking lot. "It never takes me this long to find parking at Bridgewater," he threw his arm around her and kissed the top of her silky black hair.

"Will you stop it with Bridgewater? If you like it so much, why don't you just move there?"

Not a bad idea. He knew a couple of kids from Bridgewater who gave its public school system two thumbs up. And he also knew a couple of people who lived there that commuted to New York City for work. "I might. I just might."

They entered the mall through the men's section at Macy's. It seemed that this store was always having a sale. A lady selling perfume stopped them so she could offer Rina a free sample. "How about you young man?" the blonde said to him.

"No thanks. I don't wear perfume."

"I meant some men's cologne," she laughed at his sense of humor.

"Nah, that's okay. As long as I got her, there's not much I got to do for myself," he kissed Rina on top of her silky black hair. His eyes were still open, warily keeping an eye on the blonde saleswoman.

He could tell by her smile that the saleswoman felt impressed. She said to Rina, "Don't let this one get away."

Walking into the mall, Rina suggested, "Why don't we get them his and her cologne?"

"Yeah, I was thinking about that too. But that stuff's eventually going to run out. Shouldn't we get them something a little more everlasting?"

Rina led them into stores such as *Unlimited* and *Coach*, where she suggested a coat and a bag, respectively. Danny rejected both, saying they were both way too feminine. "We could buy Sunil something else and present it together."

"We could do that," he said. "But if it's going to be a wedding present, don't you think it should be something that they can like share and use together?"

She agreed, but still bought a few items for herself from *Express*. He carried the bag for her. When he noticed that other people stared at him holding a bag from *Express*, he handed it back to her.

33

"Hey, let's stop here for a sec," he pointed to the FAO Schwartz toy store.

"Danny," she laughed. "They don't even have kids yet."

"You know I've always got to stop here," he led them in. A mother carrying two bags from the store dragged her whining son out. The kid was pointing in the direction of a life sized St. Bernard stuffed animal.

"I kind of feel sorry for the kid," Danny patted the head of the stuffed animal.

"This is expensive," she pointed to the price tag.

"I know. I wouldn't have bought it either." He felt like he was suddenly defending himself. "I guess I just can remember what it feels like to be that kid."

He forgot his defensive attitude when he noticed her glancing in the direction of the life like baby dolls. They walked through the aisle that shelved the action figures. He walked slowly so he could observe with the corners of his eyes, but he was careful not to stop and stare at one of those DC characters. Anyway, none of them resembled the original characters he had seen on television as a little kid. Usually, he would just want to see how ridiculously the new versions failed to resemble the classics.

"Why don't you get this?" she waved around a toy version of a lightsaber. She pressed a button, and it expanded into a life size weapon.

"For a wedding present?"

"No silly," she laughed. "For you! You love Star Wars."

"Yeah, but don't you think I'm getting a little old for something like that? What am I? Eight!"

"You're only as old as you want to be. Come on. I'll buy it for you."

"No. Come on. Please, don't."

"I will," she pressed her nose against his. "It's my money." No sense in arguing, he told himself. By the time they had kids, the thing would probably be worth some money.

She carried the FAO Schwarz bag too, and he did not object. Upon reaching the second level, they found themselves right in front of the food court. The salad at the mall usually came with ridiculously high price tags but an insufficient amount to be full. "Want to get some ice cream?" he said.

"Okay. Let's get a milk shake."

"What flavor?"

"Vanilla!"

He took her empty hand in his. He placed a five-dollar bill on the counter, and asked for a large vanilla milk shake with two straws. They found themselves an empty bench right in front of the balcony that overlooked the ground floor. They could see all the little people, walking in and out of the various stores. They could see a couple kissing, people arguing, and kids trying to keep up with the crowd. With the light saber handy, his lady beside him, sitting on the elevated throne, Danny could stretch his imagination so that he was a King.

"We still didn't find something for Sunil and Justine yet," she reminded him.

"We'll go to the *Wiz*," he said. "I guess maybe we can get them something like a digital camera or something. You know, so they can like capture the best moments of their lives."

"Oh yeah. That's a good idea. I don't know why I didn't think about that."

"Guess you just bring out the best in me." He brushed her hair back with his fingers. He kissed her forehead, her eyes, the tip of her nose, and finally he captured her mouth. He found her responsive and waiting, her tongue warmly greeted his. She wrapped her arms around his shoulders like he was a life preserver and she was drowning in the sea. He became oblivious that there were people around who were watching him. For all he cared, he could have been at the beach or right near a waterfall, where the only other creatures would have been birds, chirping their dulcet hymns.

"Lulu!" A discordant angry voice, unmistakably from India rudely interrupted his dream. They stared at the man who had just walked out of a shoe store. Quite not so handsome, with his wrathful countenance he seemed capable of setting whatever crossed his path on fire. His taste in clothes was obsolete: bell-bottoms and a workman's striped shirt. His almost square spectacles looked too large for his face and he had as much hair on his mustache as he did on his head. Danny grabbed Rina as if to shield her from danger. He felt ready to recollect one of his wrestling moves. The man stood there trembling, and then stormed away in the direction of Macys'.

"What the fuck was that about?" he asked her, slightly irritated.

She did not answer. She did not even look at him. Instead, her gaze was focused on the man who was storming away. Breaking out of Danny's grip, she left the bench, leaving behind her *Express* bag. The milkshake fell off the bench and spilled on the floor. "Bapu, nehi Bapu." Rina ran after the man.

Danny tried to get up, but slipping on the milkshake, he fell back onto the bench, and then on the floor. A security guard came by, asked him if he was okay, and helped him to his feet. Danny thanked the man, and grabbing the bags, he sprinted across the path Rina had gone. He knew exactly what had just occurred. He had spent too much time with Rina to know that "Lulu" was her nickname at home and that she called her father "Bapu". And he recalled that a while back, Rina told him that she had yet to tell her father about them.

He sprinted down the escalators, dodging too many slothful people who did not care to walk down the automatic stairs. He quickly looked around the shoe section and continued his frantic run. The lady selling perfume, smiled at him, but he ran past her, into the men's section, and out into the hot sunny outdoors. The

36

bright sun obstructed his vision. He just realized that in his frantic run, he had misplaced his cap. Everywhere he looked, he saw at least five different people either getting in or out of their cars. He didn't even know what car Rina's father drove, or where he parked it.

Sadly, he realized there were many things about Rina he did not know.

It had been four days since he had seen or even heard from Rina. She did not call or e-mail him. He would call, but no one would answer the phone. The answering machine had been turned off. Every night, he would drive past her house. All the lights were on and even the drapes were open. But there was no one in sight. He would feel tempted to get out of his car and knock on the front door. But someone would probably look through the peephole and see it was he. Rina would probably get a beating.

Sometime during that week, his boss had summoned him to his office. He asked Danny if everything was all right. Danny said yes. His boss told him that he noticed he had been uncharacteristically quiet lately. Danny assured him that everything was okay. Something unexpected had come up, and he was trying to cope with it. Everything would be okay soon. Really soon.

He would tell his parents that he had to work late, since he could not bear to break down in front of them while they were enjoying their meal. He would also not be ready for one of his grandfather's sporadic visits. So he would eat alone in some diner on Route 1 or Route 18. He would order a salad and fries or vegetable soup. With him would be a brochure, which recommended getaways for couples. He had enough money saved up. Maybe he would take Rina to the Bahamas in August. Or maybe he would take her to Utah to go skiing. Last time they were skiing, it was in Pennsylvania. She told him she really enjoyed it and that she wanted to do it again.

A couple three booths down celebrated a wedding anniversary. Their baby, who looked just like his father, was having a jolly time spilling his food all over the place. "Thank you," the man said to his wife, "for making me the happiest man in the world all these years."

"Thank you," she replied, "for helping me make the best mistake of my life."

Danny observed the couple kissing. The baby spilled food onto his father's head. The man laughed, cleaning out his hair. He removed the baby from the high chair and tightly hugged him.

" . . . Would you like some dessert?" the waitress broke his concentration.

"Maybe in a couple of years," he smiled at her.

"I'm sorry?"

"Maybe some other time," he placed a ten-dollar bill on the table. Smiling, he said goodnight to her, and told her that he would see her soon. Very soon!

She eventually called him on a Friday night. Lying on his bed, he tossed a baseball into the air with the TV tuned on to Wrestle Mania. He really didn't pay attention to the program, as it had been several years since he had followed this program ardently.

"Hello?"

"Danny?"

"Hey," he sat up straight, tossing the ball down on the navy blue carpet. Both of his hands grabbed the receiver.

"It's Rina." Not since college had they found the need to identify themselves when they spoke on the phone.

"Yeah, I know. Haven't talked to you in like too long. How're you doing?"

"I'm okay. You?"

"I've known better days!"

During a moment of silence, he reached into his bedside drawer where for the past several months he hid the ring, which he bought from Bridgewater. "Listen," he whispered into the phone. "There's something that I have to tell you."

"Yeah, me too." She sounded graver than he did.

"Okay, you first." He really didn't mean it, even regretted saying it. But Danny learned that old habits die-hard.

"Danny. I'm really sorry about what happened on Saturday. I didn't mean to just leave you there alone . . ."

"No worries. I'm just glad you called. That was your Dad, wasn't it?"

"Yeah," she sighed.

"He didn't know about us, did he?"

"Well, he didn't know that we were dating . . ."

"So, he didn't know, did he?"

"No!"

It all began to make sense. He had never stepped into her house. Not once. She would always ask him to pick her up at the corner of her block. He had taken the liberty to introduce her to his parents, and even his grandfather. He even took her to Sunday Mass a couple of times. But she never introduced him to her family. Coincidentally, he had bumped into her once at the supermarket, when she was with her mother. Aside from that, she had never asked him to accompany her and her family to a Hindu festival.

"Guess it must've been a real shocker for him to see some piece of white trash swap spit with his little girl."

"Yeah. He wasn't very happy about it."

Tightening his grip around the ring box, he thought about the couple in the diner. It was something about what the lady said. It was something about making the best mistake of her life. "Look, I'm really sorry that he had to find out the way he did. If I could change things, I'd . . ."

"Yeah, but you can't!"

"What's that?"

"You can't change what happened!"

"No, I can't. But I can definitely fix things. Rina, I love you!"

The silence and wait for her to respond mutually seemed to last an eternity. He could not even hear her breath on the other end of the line. "Rina? Hello? Are you there? Hello?"

"Yeah, I'm still here."

"Well?"

"Danny. You should . . ."

"I should what?"

"Look, it was . . . my Dad just isn't so used to all this . . ."

"What? Seeing his daughter kiss someone in public?"

"Not just that. It's just . . . look, we only came to America eight years ago."

"And my family came here like eighty years ago. Look, Rina, we can get through this. I'll talk to your father. I'll let him know how much you mean to me. He'll understand. He's gotta!"

"No Danny. You can't do that!"

"Sure I can," he said with inspiring confidence. "If I can handle my grandfather, I can handle anyone."

"No, you can't do that. Danny, he says if he ever sees you near me again, then he'll call the police!"

"The police!" He laughed bitterly. "What do the cops have anything to do with this? Is it like against the law to be crazy about you?"

"Danny, I'm serious. Look, my father's a really nice person. But in some cases, he just refuses to be reasonable."

"But what do the cops have anything to do with this? I mean, seriously, I can see him like point a fucking shotgun at me, but the cops? Whoa, hold up! What the hell did you exactly tell him? You made me out to be some sort of fucking jerk, didn't you? Like some sort of player, didn't you? Didn't you?"

"Danny . . ." he could hear her begin to cry. "Look, I'm really sorry . . ."

"Sounds like you're breaking up with me," he sighed. "Is this right? Your old man's making you break up with me, isn't he!"

"I'm sorry Danny," he could hear her wipe her tears. He wanted to jump in his car so he could drive to her, and hold her, and tell her everything was going to be all right. "But they're my family," she interrupted his chivalry. "I can't hurt them."

"Oh, now that makes me feel a whole lot fucking better. You're doing this for your family. Their happiness comes at my expense. You can't hurt them, but you have no problem hurting the guy who cares the most about you! Is that how it goes?"

"I'm sorry Danny!"

"You know, you're not just hurting me. You can't tell me that you're not pissed at your old man. Looks to me you care a whole not more about your next of kin than they do about you." He slammed the phone down against its cradle and fell into a deep weary slumber.

He waited for her to call back. She would call, telling him how wrong her father was, and it was time for her to stand up to him. His wait lasted for minutes, which turned into hours, which turned into days, and finally two and a half months. It felt like he had never woken from his nap. He still had her *Express* bags, which remained under his bed, unopened. Several times, he contemplated driving by her house late at night, and leaving the bags at her doorstep, along with a note that said, "I love you." He wrote her countless e-mails, but deleted before he clicked on the send button. He would pick up the phone, dial her number, hear half a ring, and then hang up.

By the time July had come, he had yet to buy a present for Sunil and Justine. Finally, he decided that he would write them a check. The two of them could figure out what to do with the money. Together!

The Hindu ceremony took place in a temple located in Bridgewater, called the Venkateswar Temple, located right down the street from Bridgewater Commons. Dutifully, Danny dressed himself in a *pajama* and a *kurta*, the traditional Bengali attire. Danny, Sunil, and three other friends from high school waited at Sunil's house, for a member of the brides' family to pick up the groom. Justine's family had sent a first cousin of her to represent them and escort Sunil to the temple. Sunil joined the cousin in the rear seat of a silver Mercedes. Danny accompanied his three other friends in a chauffeur driven BMW that closely trailed the Mercedes. The driver was an Indian. Justine mentioned a few weeks earlier that since Sunil's grandparents were coming from Kolkata, for the special occasion, her parents would try their best to make the wedding feel like it was actually occurring in India.

The friends who accompanied Danny in the BMW were Tommy Gregory, Bobby Bader, and Ryan Lowell. Tommy now worked as a mechanic. Bobby, a fellow wrestler, was in his final year of medical school. Ryan managed his family convenience store. When they drove past the mall, Tommy said, "Wow. I haven't been there since forever. Hey Dan, remember how back in high school we used to try to pick up girls there after work?"

He did remember, but he had a difficult time recollecting. What if that day he had gone shopping with Rina, he had actually convinced her to go to Bridgewater? Maybe then, he would be bringing a more original gift to the wedding. Maybe then, he would not be going to the wedding with these old chums. Only, just only had he convinced her to go to Bridgewater that day, he might not have felt so miserable right about now.

When the cars pulled up to the temple, a number of guests from the bride's side stood ready to warmly welcome the groom. Justine's mother, dressed in a sari, greeted Sunil. She placed a white marriage crown on his head and affectionately fed him rice pudding, the instant he stepped out of the Mercedes. Justine's cousin, escorted Sunil, Danny, and their three friends to a temporary room, where Sunil was instructed to sit in a throne like chair. Two smaller seats on either side of the throne, designated for Danny and the others. Several of Justine's friends and relatives came to meet and speak to Sunil. The professional photographer looked at Danny and said, "Smile. You're at a wedding, not a funeral." Danny suspected that Justine asked her parents to arrange the seating so that there would be no room for any of the groom's men's dates.

Finally, Justine's father and sisters came to escort Sunil to the wedding pandal. The pandal was fully decorated with a wide variety of flowers. A Hindu priest sat underneath the pandal, on a large piece of white cloth, and instructed Sunil to sit directly opposite him. Danny and his friends all sat on chairs that were directly behind the pandal. As Sunil repeated various Sanskrit verses that the priest dictated to him, Danny looked around the circular arrangement of chairs, each filled, with the exception of three. They were probably designated for Justine's mother, and two grandmothers, who sat in an adjacent room, waiting patiently with the bride.

He saw friends from high school, and friends from college, and people he had met at parties in New York City. Most of them dressed in suits. Some of the Indian girls his age dressed in saris, but the majority of Indian guys there, regardless of age, dressed in suits. Some of the men even dressed only in slacks and a plain shirt. It seemed like they didn't even know that they got invited for a wedding. Danny caught a glimpse of his parents, who sat right behind Sunil's father. His mother donned a red sari, her hair pulled up in a bun. His father wore suit slacks and a *kurta*, the traditional Indian top. Underneath the *kurta*, Danny could see that his father sported a tie and a dress shirt. They had brought along

43

his grandfather, who dressed strictly in a navy blue suit. His grandfather managed a glance of Danny's wandering eyes. He smiled at Danny, who pretended like he didn't see it.

Before Danny realized it, Justine's friends and sisters escorted her into the main hall of the temple. Sunil stood right outside of the pandal, holding in his hands, a garland of flowers. Tommy and Ryan shielded him from everyone's vision by concealing him with a life size piece of white cloth. Justine walked into the main hall, dressed in a red sari, her face meticulously decorated with makeup and paint. She too held a garland, and her sister helped her circle the groom three times.

Soon, Tommy and Ryan would remove the white shield. Even if he had known Justine for years, Sunil would still be in for a surprise. Justine had never looked so beautiful in her life. Sunil would be starting a new life, given new responsibilities. It would be his job to be the best husband possible to protect his bride with all his might from the cruelties of the world. In return, he got rewarded with a soul mate that came with love, acceptance, and courage, not to forget that beautiful blonde hair.

For the first time in his life, Danny admitted being jealous of his best friend.

-For Matt & Jenn Blaustein, and for Sid & Beth Singh
March 28, 2001

The Missing Link

Slowly, Gopal backed his way out of the living room congested by the Bengali men and women, who he had grown up addressing as Mesho and Mashi, like they were actually his real uncles and aunts. No one, in the midst of talking to each other, would notice his disappearance. Just as no one would bother to ask what upset him. All would assume that his sadness came from today being the second death anniversary of his mother.

A large framed picture of his mother, adorned with a white garland, rested on the floor, right underneath the wall sized bay window that would have looked into the front yard and street covered with the cars of all these mourners, had not the curtain been covering its view. In front of the picture, lay a large silver plate that housed fruits of every kind. Most people had brought flowers, and placed them on either side of the plates. His father sat next to Swapan Mesho, one of the uncles, who besides working as a private accountant by day would intermittently don the role of a part time Hindu priest. Lately, people asked him to conduct the weddings, the occasional pujas, and these death ceremonies.

Even though Gopal could not follow a word of Sanskrit, he knew that the verses uttered from the priest's mouth sounded, well, less than perfect. His older brother Shankar, and sister-in-law, Lisa, prepared the vegetarian meals in the adjacent kitchen to be distributed to all the attendees. Since getting married, Shankar rarely visited here anymore. He had moved to Chicago to work for a software company while Lisa continued to pursue her doctorate in English at the University of Chicago. So, now his father solely inhabited this large house. But it had several visitors a day, since his father's dental practice took place in the room converted from the garage.

Gopal's black denim jacket waited dutifully for him on the wooden banister of the staircase. It would shield him well from the October winds. The blue light cotton *kurta* he wore could not protect the body against cold weather. He did not bother to scoot up the stairs to his room to change into his sweats. Slipping his sock covered feet into a pair of Adidas sandals, he quietly made his way out the door.

Walking in the dark streets, he lit a Marlboro cigarette and stared into the sky as he blew smoke out of his mouth. It was not a full moon, but the stars made their presence known that night. When he was four or five, right before he started nursery school, his mother read him a story about a coyote that stole the light away during the night, and to compensate, he put stars in the sky so that the night would not be completely dark. "How did the coyote know that the stars won't fall from the sky?" he asked his mother while she tucked him into bed. She said that the coyote had used a special kind of superglue.

He preferred to mourn alone. The relationship that he had had with his mother could not be appreciated fully by anyone, not his father, his brother, probably not his sister-in-law, and definitely none of those uncles and aunts. Undeniably, Shankar, seven years older than Gopal, was their father's son, whereas Gopal formed a more intimate bond with their mother. By his thirteenth birthday, Shankar stood close to six feet tall, and excelled at soccer and basketball, being the only non-black kid to make the junior high basketball team. Gopal would grow to be at most five foot three inches, and other than baseball, he displayed little interest in sports, though in gym class, he always managed to run the mile in less than six minutes. Instead he indulged in playing the violin, an art that he had been introduced to by his mother, who besides being a well-respected pediatrician, was also a gifted violinist. From the time he was four, Gopal trained with several violin teachers, concentrating on classical southern Indian music. He performed at Carnegie Hall and for his school orchestra. At sixteen, he had his Arangetram, a musical graduation. Family friends, colleagues of his parents, and even some buddies from school attended.

At night, when his father would take Shankar to the park to kick around the soccer ball or shoot some hoops, Gopal would practice his violin, and then pester his mother to tell him stories about Bhim, the Indian mythological version of Hercules. To Gopal, Bhim was the most fascinating character, since it was his style to protect the weak, and humiliate those who abused their power. Due to his size, Gopal really could not defend himself much while growing up, and because of the large age gap, he did not have easy access to his big brother for protection.

Right after his family moved from Flushing to their new home on Long Island before seventh grade, Gopal became the easy target of this bully named Will Young. Will, who was not only tall for his age, but also slightly overweight, would seize every opportunity to humiliate Gopal. After Gopal would perform one of his songs, Will would say, "This is America you Gandhi idiot. Play some real music."

Once in Social Studies class, Gopal had to do a presentation on his own culture, and he brought in a picture of the deity Ganesh. Will said, "What type of cave people worship a fucking elephant?" All this Gopal, endured with patience, but one time during lunch, when Will called out to him, "Hey Gopal, tell your mother that I'll be five minutes late meeting her tonight", Gopal decided that enough was enough. Will's cronies found it quite hilarious.

Gopal slowly walked over to Will's table. He picked a Hostess cupcake off of Will's tray, and then shoved it right against Will's forehead. "Yo, what the fuck, I'll kill you," Will violently rose from his chair, but the gym teacher interfered just in time, sending them both to get reprimanded by the vice-principal. Yet Will's tortures did not cease.

One day, right after the last bell of school had rung, Gopal maneuvered his way through the crowded hallways, when it happened that the case of his violin slammed into Will's knee. "Sorry" he said and made his way out of the school heading home. Will, ever looking for an excuse to pick a fight, followed Gopal with two of his friends. He grabbed Gopal by his jacket, and pushed him a few feet. "Why'd you hit me for asshole!"

"Sorry, it was just a mistake!"

Will then shoved him up against the grass, and Gopal lost the grip of his violin case. "You're making too many mistakes. Someone should teach you some manners." Will kicked the violin case, sending it onto the sidewalk. Enraged, Gopal charged at Will, but in that situation, it did not matter how big the size of the fight inside the dog was, since this time the opponent was a bear. Will grabbed a hold of Gopal's hair, and held him at arm's length away. Poor Gopal took punches into the air, his short arms not being able to come in contact with Will's body. Will carried with him the confidence of a Greek god who knew not an enemy in the world. A small crowd of commuters gathered around to watch the bullying. "Fuck that Patel up," yelled out Tom Campbell, one of Will's cronies who had all the marks of someone entering adolescence. You know, the changing voice, the extra long arms.

Gopal's plight would be short, since riding his Mongoose red bike on the street came Jason Hegudus, another tall kid, who had the reputation of being the best baseball player of his age group. A white boy, Jason spent countless hours on the basketball courts but would never step foot inside a hockey rink, would listen devotedly to rap music, but would not care for heavy metal. Jason batted clean up, stole a lot of bases, and could adroitly hold his own whether he was pitching, playing shortstop, or placed in centerfield. He had an insanely quick pitching arm, and as of last week, only Will hit a more than a single off of him. Next to Jason came his black friend Tyrone, riding his blue GT Pro performer bike. Jason hopped off his bike, broke through the small crowd, and grabbed Will's hand using pressure points, forcing Will to release his grip on Gopal's hair. "What the fuck seems to be the problem," Jason said to Will. "Leave him alone!"

It took Will a few moments to respond after retreating a step. "He uhm, he he . . . . . .he . . ."

"He what?"

"He banged my knee with that big box."

Jason took a step closer to Will, as he stripped himself of his backpack and jacket. "It was a mistake," Jason shoved Will sending him back a few feet. "This is on purpose!" Jason then hurled his fist right onto Will's nose, sending him on his back on the grass. Blood poured incessantly down from Will's nose. Ouch, Gopal thought to himself. Try as he may, he could not conceal his smile.

Jason's friend Tyrone helped Gopal gather his stuff, while Jason spoke down to Will, "See that's when you're supposed to fight back. You get the difference now or you need me to show you again!"

To Gopal's disappointment, Will waived his hand as if to say sorry.

"That was no accident," Tyrone said to Will. "How come you ain't fighting back? You a pussy, you dumb ogre. I ever hear you touch Gopal again Jason's punch is gonna feel like a blowjob from your Momma." Tyrone rushed over to Will and feigned a kick to his ribs, causing Will to fall again in fear as he tried to get himself up.

Turning to Tom Campbell, Jason did not attempt any physical assault. Why should he! Tom stood a head shorter. Instead, he said to him, "My man's last name ain't Patel, it's Ghosh! You got that?" Tom nodded timidly. Jason told Tom to spell Ghosh, but Gopal tugged on Jason's jacket, and the two friends escorted Gopal home, carrying him on the handlebars of Tyrone's bike.

Gopal spent the rest of high school free of any worries about being bullied. He ran cross-country simply to be able to mention in his college applications that he had participated in a sport. But for the better part, his extra-curricular activities entailed student government and the school orchestra. He would not date any one in high school, until in his senior year, when Elizabeth Roberto asked him to be her date to the prom. During prom weekend, she admitted to him that she had a crush on him throughout the year, but she finally found the courage to tell him so. He told her that he was flattered but it didn't make sense to pursue a relationship. With her going away to the University of Virginia while he'd attend Swarthmore, a long distance relationship just wouldn't work.

At Swarthmore, he would not be involved in any serious relationship either. He would go home to Long Island every few weeks, where he would encounter altercations with his father who demanded to know what possessed Gopal to major in political science rather than say, biochemistry or engineering. Shankar had majored in biology at MIT, and even got accepted into medical school. But he deferred that in favor of working as a sales rep for a pharmaceutical company, and eventually gone on to earn his MBA. Gopal would be the second son to disappoint his father. His mother, on the other hand, applauded his choice of a major, and told him that she would be proud of him as long as he put his best effort into what he was doing. During the summers, he worked as an assistant to a Jesuit priest who sought to restructure the library systems for Catholic schools that had a large concentration of students from lower class families. By his junior year, Gopal earned a rather high score on the LSATs, and by the beginning of his senior year, he started to fill out applications to law schools.

The tragic day came that October, when he had come home for the annual Durga Puja. Often enough, he heard his father complain as to how Durga Puja in the States could not compare to those held in India, but nevertheless was still fun because it was one of the few events that united the Bengalis of New York City. As usual the Puja occurred at the Gujarati Samaj in Fresh Meadows. Gopal declined to do a violin performance that year, as law school applications and his senior year thesis kept him busy. But he had a good time reuniting with all the Bengali kids he had grown up with. Shankar appeared, with his then new bride Lisa. Rishi, a senior at Penn studying physics, was looking into PhD programs. Sonya, who went to Cooper Union, planned to become an investment banker after graduation. All of a sudden, Gopal began to feel nauseous. Others commented that he did not look so well. He began to run a fever. He told his parents that he felt ill. "Can you tough it out for a few more hours?" His father asked him.

"Baba, I don't feel good at all."

"That's ok," his mother said to his father. "I'll take him home. Shankar and Lisa will bring you home."

Gopal's mother drove him home in their Honda Accord. On a Saturday night in October, traffic did not congest the Long Island Expressway. But the drive home still felt too long, and he slightly rolled down the window to feel the comfort of the wind.

When they finally reached his house, he rushed out of the car, even before his mother could shut off the ignition. He quickly found his house key in the pocket of his denim coat, and rushed into the half bathroom in the corridor. Falling to his knees against the marble tiles, he violently vomited into the toilet bowl. Slowly rising to his feet, he stared at himself in the mirror, and saw that he was tearing.

His mother told him to go to his room and change into something comfortable. He kept his socks on, but slipped into flannel pants and a Swarthmore sweatshirt. He slipped into bed underneath the quilt and must've dozed off for a few hours. When he awoke, he did feel a bit better, and saw his mother lying next to him in bed. He had fallen asleep in her arms, as he had

51

often done as a toddler when Shankar would scare him with horror stories that he picked up at Boy Scouts' camp.

"Are you feeling better?" She asked him.

"Yeah, kinda. What's up with me?"

"I think you got a virus of some sort. You'll live."

"Thanks. I'm actually kind of hungry. Say, do we got some of that tomato soup?"

"I think so. If we don't, I'll just stop by the grocery store to get some."

"No Ma, you don't have to do that."

"Don't worry Beta," she assured him. "I have to do the groceries anyway. But tell me. How's Rishi doing?"

"I think he wants to go to Cornell for graduate school. But he's also thinking about USC since his girlfriend wants to go back home to the west coast."

"Who's his girlfriend?"

"I think some South Indian girl."

His mother made a curious smile. "Tell me something. And be honest. Are you seeing anyone now?"

"Uhm. Why?"

"Sonya's single. Would you be interested in going on a date with her?"

He sat himself up and glanced over to his bedside table. On it, lay a biography of Napoleon, next to a framed picture of him, and some of his best friends from Swarthmore: Jorge, a Puerto Rican from Texas, Justin, a music major from New Jersey, and Rubina, a Pakistani Muslim girl from Pennsylvania. In the picture, Rubina had her arms wrapped around Gopal's waist, her chin resting against his shoulder, her cheek, resting against his. "Ma," he said, "there's something that I've been meaning to tell you for a while."

"Yes, Beta, what is it?"

"Uhm, can we eat first?"

They made their way down to the kitchen, but found nothing good to eat. His mother said that she would be right back, that she was going to head to the grocery store to pick up a few things. Gopal offered to accompany her, but she told him that it would be better for him to stay in. He offered again, but she insisted that he stay inside and rest it up a bit. Gopal did not argue, figuring that he would need to garner all his strength to tell her what he wanted to tell her.

But he would never be able to tell her. His mother never returned that day. She got killed in a car accident, when a speeding drunk driver had passed a red light, and drove directly into the driver's side of his mother's Honda Accord, resulting in an instantaneous death. And he never could tell his mother, or anyone else, what exactly was going through his mind then.

While he reminisced the days of his youth and the last hours that he spent with his mother, Gopal had inadvertently walked to his old high school. He made his way to the empty baseball field, where he made himself comfortable on top of the visitor's benches. He lit himself another cigarette and glanced and pulled out his cell phone. Melissa had yet to call. Was something the matter? In the past two days, he called her five times, but she had yet to reply. Rather unusual of her. A few weeks ago he told her about the death anniversary of his mother, and she promised to come. They had not spoken in little over a week. Not wanting to be alone anymore for the night, he began to redial Melissa's number, yet again reached her voicemail.

After graduating from Swarthmore, Gopal's desire to attend law school abated. Instead, he accepted a job as a community organizer for a non-profit organization that dedicated itself to helping victims of domestic violence, mainly victims of alcoholics. While his office lay on the upper east side of Manhattan, he found a subsidized studio on Morningside Heights. After nine months of work, he met Melissa. She had come in there to interview for a SAS programming position. Being the third and last person to meet with her, he walked into the room. He stared at her for two minutes before introducing himself. "Melissa? Hi. Gopal!"

"Nice to meet you Gopal." She had a nice grip, cordial and friendly.

"You've got an impressive resume," he told her. "Bachelors and Masters from Tufts. And four years of I-banking. And you want to work for a non-profit? You're aware we can't afford to pay you as well, right?"

"Yes," she replied. "After four years of working the corporate world, I can honestly tell you that money's not on my list of priorities. Before I got lured by the glamour of Wall Street, I was at Tufts specializing in child development. I think that I finally found my calling to work in the non-profit sector." She went on about how right after she obtained her Master's, a friend of hers from undergrad helped her obtain an interview with a financial firm in the city, and with the money being so good, she found it difficult to say no. After several years, she found herself unfulfilled, and when she heard about this job, she applied with the hope of being happy. He liked her answers, and put in a good word for her. She got hired within the next week.

On her second day of work, he took her out to dinner at the Indian restaurant, Baluchi's in midtown. She asked him for recommendations, and he told her to try the chicken masala. "How long have you been living on 57th street?" He asked her.

"A little less than a year," she said. "Before that, I was living with some friends in Battery Park."

"Were you there right after college?"

"No. I actually stayed with my parents in Flushing for a few months. It's a little over a year come to think about it."

"What part of Flushing are you from?"

"My parents live right off of Bowne Street."

54

"No way," he told her, "I practically grew up on Franklin Ave. It's right by this Hindu temple."

"Yeah," she said. "I know exactly which one you're talking about. "I grew up two blocks away from there."

They had much more in common. Both of them had older siblings who were Yankee fans, and neither one could fathom how anyone growing up a subway station stop away from Shea Stadium could root for the Bronx Bombers. "I make it a point to see the Mets at least twice a year," she told him.

"You're lucky," he said. "I think the last time I was even at Shea Stadium was like when my mom bought me tickets for my tenth birthday."

"Wow, that was like ages ago!"

"Tell me about it. That's like when they still had Daryl Strawberry and Keith Hernandez."

"Tell you what," she said. "We'll go once next season starts."

They would hang out much more often after work. Often times, she would visit friends who were doing graduate work at Columbia, and she would stop by his studio on Morningside Heights. Together, they would go to the local Blockbuster to rent a movie like *For Love of the Game* or *X-Men*. She would applaud him when she heard him play the violin. She herself used to play the piano during elementary school, but she really did not get along too well with her instructor, who happened to be a nun. "Anytime I pressed the wrong note, she'd slap my hand." Had she had a better instructor, she would have stuck with it.

Once he met up with his friend Jorge from Swarthmore who decided to spend a three-day furlough in New York City. Gopal decided that they should go see a Broadway show. Coincidently, they had run into Melissa during their pre-show dinner. "Hey," she approached them. "What are you doing here?"

"We're gonna catch a show. Jorge, Melissa. Melissa, my friend Jorge from college. Wanna join us."

"Only for a little while. I'm meeting my sister in a few minutes."

Jorge did most of the talking, and he told Melissa a few tales of Gopal's idiosyncrasies in college. "My man here would always have his CD player on, and it was always tuned into something like Ravi Shankar or something like that. Occasionally, just occasionally, you'd hear him turn on the Beatles. He's a heart breaker too. All four years this babe Rubina was practically throwing herself at him, and he kept her waiting and waiting . . . Say Gopal, what ever . . ."

"Melissa," Gopal interrupted him. "Where are you going with your sister?"

Melissa glanced at her wristwatch. "Oh. Thanks for reminding me. I gotta go. Nice meeting you."

Jorge observed her figure as she made her way out of the diner. "Not bad man, why don't you go for her?"

"C'mon man, she's like four years older than me."

"So what! Did you check out that body of hers?"

"Yo c'mon man, hold it right there."

"Shit, if you're that defensive about her, you must really like her."

Gopal stared out the window and watched Melissa slowly disappear into the crowded streets of midtown New York. "Y'know man, I do wonder why girls can't be more like Melissa."

For several months, because of their schedules, Melissa and Gopal saw each other only during work meetings and occasionally lunch. Melissa analyzed a lot of data, while Gopal travelled to all parts of the city to schedule and organize events, and recruit new counselees who got victimized by alcoholics. One day, Melissa came into his office so that she could collect new spreadsheets that he had put together.

"Hey, what's up," she said to him.

"Work, work, and work. You?"

"You said it. We haven't hung out in a while. Wanna do something, let's see, no, not next Saturday, but the one after that?"

"I'd love to," he shook his head. "But I gotta spend time with my family then. It's my mom's death anniversary."

"Oh! I'm sorry."

"Yeah, but hey, you wanna come over to my dad's house that day. I could use the company then."

"Yeah, sure, I think I can make it over then."

A few days later, Gopal received an email from a friend inviting him to attend a private concert at Bryant Park. So he invited Melissa to come with him, who said she'd get back to him by the end of the day. Towards the end of the day, he stopped by her desk, and hopped on top of it. "So, whatcha say."

"Oh, yeah, sorry, I can't make it today."

"Oh c'mon, I've got a spare ticket."

"What about your dad?"

"Yeah right, that's a laugh. My dad at a classical concert."

"Sorry, I just can't make it today. But I'll probably come to your place on Saturday."

"But not tonight?"

"Sorry Kiddo."

"Fine, but you owe me, remember that!"

He was sort of relieved that Melissa did not accompany him to the concert. It was not that great. For the next two days Melissa did not show up at work. Curious as to why, he called her, only to reach her voicemail. "Where's Melissa?" He asked Wanda, the secretary.

"Oh, she quit."

"What, when did this happen?"

"Two days ago. She called in and submitted her resignation."

"What, what brought this on?"

"She said that she got an offer from some bank."

Gopal stared at the blank ugly wall. As if abruptly, he realized the ugliness and depressing ambience of the office building he worked in. He could begin to feel how prisoners with a long sentence felt when confined to a building that taxpayers refused to ameliorate. It all began to make sense. More than likely, Melissa had lost a job with a financial firm, and took a job here in the interim to get some pocket change. What was it with women he cared for making abrupt departures from his life?

"What a piece of garbage!"

He didn't realize that his final thought was uttered until Wanda said to him, "Oh come on honey, you know you don't mean that. If you want a date, why don't you just ask her?"

"Huh?

Wanda stared at him like a fortuneteller. She smiled to say, "I told you so". "Oh come on Honey, it's so obvious that you're in love with her."

"What're you talking about?"

"Don't try to play dumb with me Honey. You think I didn't see you that day when Paul from accounting whistled at her when she walked by and you told him that if he ever did that again that you were going to kill him?"

"When was this?" He honestly did not recall such an event.

"Ok Honey, play dumb if you want to, but, I say let her know how you feel about her!

Wanda, the firm's gossip columnist, enjoyed adding her own twists and turns to simple events. But she did hit the target with one thing. How much he loved Melissa.

Enough was enough. Still sitting on top of the benches on the baseball field, Gopal knew that the guests at his dad's house had yet to notice his absence. No one called his cell phone to inquire about his whereabouts.

He lit yet another cigarette and then decided to walk in the direction of his dad's house, a block away from the bus stop. At first he intended to take the bus into Kew Gardens, but then thought better of it. On Saturdays neither the Q45 bus nor the F train provided much reliability.

So instead, he dug his hands into his pockets to find the keys to his dad's Celica.

It waited for him on the streets. After starting it, he let it warm up for about two minutes, slipping a Bangles CD into the car's music system. He chose to take the LIE instead of the local roads because he did not have the patience to deal with traffic lights on every single block. The ride felt rather quick, and he soon found himself on Northern Boulevard, keeping a careful eye on the radar detector as he gradually accelerated. He made it past the Queens Borough Bridge into Manhattan in no time.

When he made it to the Columbus Circle area, he pulled into a familiar garage operated by a Bangladeshi businessman. He handed the keys to the attendant and spoke to him in Bengali briefly before heading to 8th Avenue, the direction of Melissa's apartment building. The lobby looked like it belonged to some five star hotels on Madison Avenue. He walked through the revolving doors and approached the male receptionist, a young Hispanic male probably in his early twenties.

"Hey, I'm here to see Melissa Perrotta. She lives in 22B."

"I'm sorry Sir, but she left around three this afternoon."

"What do you mean she left? She'll be back right."

"I mean she went out. Yes, I think that she will be back. She made no mention of going away or nothing of that sort."

Gopal nodded his head and headed outside. He lit another cigarette, and walked across the street where he happened to be standing right in front of a closed bakery. He stared vigilantly at Melissa's building for about half an hour when he finally noticed her. Well, he heard her voice from the other side of 57th street. She sported a black glittering dress and held hands with a handsome guy who appeared just less than six feet tall, and had brown hair.

Right in front of her building, they stopped, and he could see Melissa stare into the guy's eyes. She stepped up to kiss him on the mouth. This kiss looked long and passionate. Gopal could tell even from across the street.

Watching the strange man press his body against hers, feel her all over, familiar rage from high school resurfaced when Will Young would flagrantly violate his privacy. But now, there was no Jason Hegudus to watch his back.

Disappointed, Gopal turned around ready to walk back to the garage, but then he heard Melissa say "Bye." Bingo. He turned around, and saw the guy slowly leave the building and walk back in the direction that he had come from as Melissa made the move into her building.

Gopal rushed across the street, not heeding the red light intended for pedestrians. "Melissa," he called out. "Melissa, wait, wait!"

Melissa turned around and stared abruptly at him. "Gopal. What're you doing here?" She did not seem happy to see him, he could tell. Or at least that's how he felt.

"Melissa, look, I've been calling you for a while. Why haven't you been calling me back? That's not like you."

"I've been a bit busy," she said. "I just needed a break from things."

She saw him huffing and puffing, grasping his knees as he struggled to catch his breath. "Maybe you should cut back on those cancer sticks."

"Melissa, who was that guy?"

60

"Someone my sister set me up with. Why?"

"Just curious. Was he the reason you haven't been calling me back?"

She shrugged her shoulders. "Maybe! I guess."

"Did you even have any intention of calling back? Did you even have any intention of saying goodbye, or was that it? Once Wall Street rehired you, you had no more need for the little people who waste their lives away working for nothing?"

"Look, I didn't mean to just blow you off if that's what you mean!"

"Melissa today was my mom's death anniversary. You said that you'd try to make it, and then you don't call or nothing."

The anger from her face slowly diminished and took the form of a guilty look. "Oh shit. Gopal, I'm sorry."

Gopal did his best to fight his tears. "You're sorry? Melissa, I really needed you tonight."

"Gopal. I have a boyfriend!" It sounded like a dismissal for him to leave. She did not welcome his advances.

"Yeah, and I don't care. I mean I do, but look I really need to talk to you. I drove all the way from Long Island to see you. Can't you just hear me out?"

"Okay, so what is it that you have to say?"

He grabbed her right hand with both of his. She stared at him awkwardly, but did not attempt to break away. "Look, Melissa, I'm being honest. What I feel for you now I haven't felt for a woman in a really long time. Two years . . ."

"Look Gopal, I'm flattered and all but even if I wasn't seeing someone I can't see you and me together."

"You can't?"

"No, I mean I could see you as a brother . . ."

His heart started beating faster and faster. "Melissa, can you just shut up for like two minutes and hear me out."

"What?"

"I'm gay!" For the first time he admitted this to anyone other than himself.

Now undeniably, Melissa felt total shock. "What! Are you sure?"

"Surer than anything I've ever been about in my life."

"How long have you known?"

"Since junior year in college. Maybe even longer. Junior high maybe." He could no longer hold it in. He began to sob heavily. "I was about to tell my mother a few years ago, and then she got killed."

She embraced him like a little brother, and with her bare fingers she wiped away the tears from his eyes. She brought him up to her apartment, a nicely furnished junior one bedroom. Her window had a nice view of the Hudson River and of New Jersey. He sat down on her couch under a framed autographed poster of Keith Hernandez, as she made tomato soup for him in the kitchen. By the time the soup was ready and she brought it over to him, he gradually drifted off to sleep. She sat down next to him and wrapped her arm around him, placing his head on her shoulder, whispering a promise into his ear that she would accompany him to classical concerts, and that next baseball season she would definitely take him out to Shea Stadium. But first he'd have to promise her to quit smoking.

-For Brian Jo
11.19.2003

Dada is Watching

He's not really my brother. He's not my cousin. Our families aren't even related. But my parents always insisted that I address Rana as Rana Dada or Rana Da, as Bengali custom dictates an older brother or brother figure should be addressed. The funny part is that since my name is Rana too, I became known as Chhoto Rana, Bengali for little Rana, and then I eventually acquired the nickname as Chhoto. When I was younger, I mean, really young, I must've been three or four, I didn't mind it! After I started school, I figured that I could simply call him Rana because in New York all my friends who had older brothers simply addressed their siblings by their first names. But my parents will not let me skip that part of the tradition.

After a while, I stop protesting, probably because I don't mind Rana being my surrogate older brother. One day, I run down 41st street from St. Michael's to my parent's home on the corner of Parson's Boulevard crying because the third graders won't let me play basketball with them. They say I suck. It so happens that Rana's mom, who I call Shibi Mashi, is having tea with my mom at that moment. When they find out why I am crying, Shibi Mashi tells Rana, and every afternoon, Rana takes me with him to play basketball with his junior high friends at Kissena Park. Most of his playmates are black and there are a few Latinos and Whites. Whenever they pick teams, his friends make sure to pick me first, and they teach me to play. In no time, I am playing superior b-ball with the kids my age.

Whenever my family gets invited to his family's home for dinner, Rana lets me to hang out in his bedroom where he sports an awesome collection of rap and hip-hop albums, and comic books. He lets me play tapes of LL Cool J on his boom box while I lay on his carpeted floor and read about the latest adventures of the Green Arrow or the Hulk. That must be how I acquired my taste for hip-hop. Thanks to him, I am always aware of the latest rap songs that were coming out, and I knew how to talk in slang and not to come across as a poser when I did it.

When the Bengali community has cultural festivals in Queens like the Durga Puja or Saraswati Puja, they often rent the auditorium of a public junior high. This precedes the time when the Gujarati Samaj becomes the conventional avenue for housing the functions. That's when all the Bengali kids hang out with each other, and I usually try to hang out with Rana. I remember one year, I must've been in fourth grade, and Rana isn't there at the Puja yet. This one dork that is a lot older than me starts to call me names and pushes me around, but more in an intellectual style. He's one of those geeks who wears those five inch thick glasses and like a math and chess champion who was a Westinghouse finalist and is on his way to study at Caltech but is too modern to be talking in Bengali or wear Indian clothes. Despite being much smaller, I want to retaliate physically. He is a wimp, but still he is older than me, and could probably take me. I push the dork, who simply pushes me back into the lockers. Finally Rana appears and I'm reminded about times when the Fonz shows up to bail Ritchie Cunningham out of trouble. By this time, Rana is in tenth grade. I am thinking that he is going to finish the dork off for me, but he just pulls me away and says, "Don't mess with him. Only way he could ever get laid is if he says, 'I'm a US Citizen.'" This dork has no comeback, and the funny part is that Rana Da's prediction does eventually come true, but perhaps you'll read about that in another story.

By the time I am in junior high and develop my first crush, I of course tell Rana about it and he gives me advice on how to act. He teaches me to dance. This guy is my hero. To me he is invincible and the guy who can take all the problems away. By the time I am in seventh grade, he is a senior at Stuyvesant High School, and on

64

his way to the University of Michigan, where he plans to study finance. I even ride in the car when his mom and his uncle drive him to Michigan his freshman year.

Right when high school starts you develop your reputation and your identity that most sticks with you for the next four years. And I become the Indian kid who indulges in black culture, wears extra large clothes, sags his pants, plays basketball, and listens to rap music. Most of my friends at school are black and by the way I act, most people mistake me for being a Latino. Maybe it also could be because I date a Puerto Rican girl for almost two years. By the end of eighth grade, my father expires, losing his battle to lymphoma. My dad's business partner cheats my mother and me out of my Dad's share of the pharmacy. My mother is forced to work full time at the bank on Kissena Boulevard, past the Queens Library and Post Office. I grow into an angry kid, complaining how unfair it was for a kid to lose his father so young. I gather a group of friends, and armed with baseball bats and hammers and spray paint, we vandalize the Mercedes that my dad's ex-business partner recently purchases. We do it one Friday night. All of us dress in ski caps and hooded sweatshirts. By the time we're done, the car suffers much abuse. This type of wanton destruction of property becomes a trademark retribution for anyone who crosses our paths. We finally realize that we go too far when we spray paint the local firehouse with our posse's insignia after one of the fire fighters calls us a bunch of good for nothing punks. We dissolve our gang when we hear that the police are looking for us.

In school, I'm no angel either. I get easily provoked, ever looking for a reason to get into a fight. Towards the middle of my freshman year, my grades begin to slip and altogether I stop caring about my schoolwork. Only thing I'm passionate about is basketball, but my coach receives a note that I may be in danger of losing my spot on the team due to a decline in grades.

When people provoke me, I don't have the mental acumen that will have words do the wounding. Instead, I retaliate quite often and end up getting suspended. Towards the end of my freshman year I earn my third suspension for blackening the eye of a kid who steps on my sneakers. My guidance counselor calls my mom into school and informs her that if I want to enroll next year as a sophomore, then I will have to attend summer school. Throughout this meeting, my mom keeps a calm composure, but on the ride home, she gives me a scolding that can only be felt in her native Bengali. "Your father suffered so much during his last few years. Now he can see everything and he sees you screwing your life up. Do you want his suffering to continue? You selfish beast." The guilt I briefly feel is quickly forgotten when she continues to berate me in Bengali. And it just goes on and on.

That evening, Rana Da stops by. He is home from college, and interning at an investment bank somewhere in Wall Street. He has a basketball, and takes me to Kissena Park for a game of one on one. I start off by showing off how good I am at foul shooting. No matter the angle on the court, I aim for the basket and swish, it goes in. Then I dribble the ball through my legs, approach him, and toss him the ball. "You know," I say to him, "they say I'm so good on the courts that you may as well call me Arjun." Arjun is the hero of India's greatest story, Mahabharat. Ma has tried forever to get me to read it, but I rather opt for my comic books.

Rana Da bounces the ball twice. "Arjun? Nah, you ain't no Arjun. You're more like Abhimanyu."

"Who the hell's that?"

"That was Arjun's cocky kid. He was way better than Arjun."

"Yeah, cool, thanks."

"I don't mean that in a good way," Rana Da says. "The kid was so cocky that he thought he didn't need no one watching his back. Then you know what happened?"

66

"Nah, what?"

"He went into a formation too quickly without waiting for his backup. Then he got ganged up on and killed. If you think you don't need no one watching your back then you better be a whole lot better than Abhimanyu." He tosses me that ball. It's a challenge for a one on one match.

I'm good, I'm the best in my class, but against, him, I still suck. He constantly fakes me out, dribbling the ball between his legs, around me. His lay ups are all too natural, and he makes them look too easy. Still, I don't get intimidated, and I manage to flaunt some of my own tricks. The game goes on for hours. He wins. We're both drenched with sweat and we sit down on the bench. "I remember when you couldn't even dribble the ball," he laughs.

"That was a long time ago." I cover my face in my soaked t-shirt.

"Wasn't that long ago. Back then you were just pathetic. But you kept at it. Now you can almost dust me off. Almost!"

I don't even look at him when he says this. I shake my head and say "Oh God, what're you gonna give me that 'you can do anything you set your mind to so get your life in order' speech."

"I think someone better. Might as well be me."

"Look man, I can take care of myself."

He hops off the bench and positions himself so he can look directly at me, though I'm doing my best to avoid eye contact. "I don't think you can. With the way you're doing in school, what're you gonna end up doing? I can tell you this man, you're not heading for the NBA. You can't even beat me."

"Look man," I get up off the bench. I'm ready to head home. I was already lectured once today. I'm not in the mood for it again. "I don't need to hear this shit, especially from someone like you. You're not my father. So fuck off." I attempt to walk away, but he grabs me by my t-shirt and shoves me back onto the bench. He has a good grip. I can tell that he spends time at the gym.

"First of all, don't ever tell me to fuck off again. It's a warning and the last one you'll ever get. I may not be your father, but I am your big brother, and you better fucking listen to me because I'm going to say this once." We've play fought several times before, but by the way he looks at me, I can tell that he is not playing. "Look, I know it's been rough on you with your dad passing away and all. You think it's a walk in the park for your mother? Now she's a single parent and got a lot more shit to carry on her shoulders. You think you're making things any easier for her! Do you, you selfish fucking brat piece of shit! Fucking straighten out or I'll make sure your mom's got one less thing to worry about!" He then grabs me by my t-shirt and pulls me up off the bench. "Your dad didn't die on purpose. Mine walked out on me and my mom and who knows what girl friend or mistress he's living with now or which one of his friends' wives he's banging. I got a reason to hate my dad. You don't. Treat him better. Not the way you'd treat my dad."

We shoot hoops for a little while longer and then I rush home to my mom, and touch her feet. I apologize for not being a model son, and promise that I will do better. I keep my promise and to pay for summer school, I get a job as a bike messenger. For the remainder of high school, I stay out of trouble and do well in school. After school, when I'm not at basketball practice, I find work at a comic book shop to help my mom with the bills. That discipline I develop in working to help Ma out with the bills saves my life because one day, while I'm at Midtown Comics, a few of my friends I used to hang out with mug an old man and steal his wallet hoping to use that to repay their outstanding debt to a ruthless cocaine dealer. Within days, the cops apprehend them. If it wasn't for Rana Da's guidance, I fear that I might have been one of those delinquents, and there is no way I'd be able to hug my Mom from a jail cell. I graduate high school and think about how Rana Da was instrumental in turning my life around for the better. And I begin to wonder if I could ever be as good a big brother as he has been.

By the time I enroll in college, Rana Da moves back to New York. He takes a job at a bank in midtown and rents an apartment on the west side, somewhere in between Penn Station and Times Square. I don't go away to school. Instead, I play basketball for a small school up in Westchester. After a semester I choose to transfer to NYU since it's close to home. And just a year ago, my mom got a full time job there in the financial aids office. So that helps out with a break in tuition.

I choose to study History along with Creative Writing. By my second semester in college, Rana Da begins to see this beautiful Indian girl named Seema who is doing her Master's in International Affairs at Columbia University. Her father, an Indian diplomat is on a two-year assignment in New York. Rana Da meets her at a United Nations gathering, and they begin to see each other exclusively. Within nine months of their courtship, Seema's dad's posting comes to and end, and he is scheduled to transition to Spain for two years. Seema wants to stay behind, both because of Rana Da and her education. So, Seema's parents propose that their daughter should wed Rana Da because they seem to be in love and also they will feel reassured that their daughter is in good hands. Rana Da and his mom readily agree.

I still remember the night he called my dorm room with the news. "Hey buddy," he says, "guess what, I'm getting married."

"Hey, that's awesome. When is it, in a year."
"Uhm, no. In three weeks."
"Three weeks," I can't even begin to tell you how shocked I feel. "She pregnant?"

"No," he laughs over the phone. Obviously, I'm not the first of his friends to ask him this question today. "Her parents just want it to be over before they leave for Spain."

For an impromptu wedding, it is pretty nice. The reception takes place in the same place where all the Bengali weddings, anniversary and graduation parties take place. The Bombay Palace on Northern Boulevard in Queens. The couple doesn't even go on a honeymoon. The following Monday, Rana Da goes back to work and Seema resumes her classes at Columbia. Within months, Seema earns her Master's and she begins work at a boutique management-consulting firm in midtown. A few months afterwards, Rana Da and Seema purchase a one-bedroom co-op on 53rd street. Their new place that they call home is convenient as it is walking distance to both their jobs.

Things go well for Rana Da. He abandons any aspirations of pursuing an MBA since he gets promoted to Vice President in minimal time. Seema enjoys her job, and she keeps active in extra-curricular activities. Oh, I forgot to mention this. Before her wedding, she won the Miss India New York pageant. That itself got her involved in lots of social scenes and charities.

On a sunny spring afternoon I am sitting on the grass underneath a tree in Union Square Park reading Descartes for a philosophy course. I begin to ponder about my future. There is only a year and a half to go when I become a college graduate and escape the cushion of academia. If I'm lucky, I'll be half the success that my older brother is.

Besides studying at NYU, I also enroll in hip-hop classes. There I befriend Farhad Islam, an American kid whose parents come from Kashmir. If you follow track and field closely enough, then you most probably have heard of Farhad. He's a nationally ranked runner. A few years ago, he almost even made the American Olympic team. He is originally from Florida, and in between high school and college he took a year off to

70

train. He went to UC San Diego but moved to New York to pursue an acting career after his athletic one came to an abrupt end. At NYU, he takes part time theatre and film classes. To help pay bills, he takes a job as a part time dance instructor. "You got good moves," Farhad says to me. "But try to stay in rhythm." Since he teaches me dancing, I teach him boxing. Another time, I'm working out at the gym sparring with Farhad, and I manage to drive him up against a wall, and take lethal punches at exposed parts of his torso, protected only by the pads. "Wow Chhoto," he says, tossing his arm over my shoulders. "You got into lots of fights, didn't you?"

"Some. Why?"

"Cause you got all the instincts of a street fighter. It would've been awesome if you got involved with an instructor when you were younger. You probably could've made the Olympics."

Farhad likes that boxing is my passion, so the two of us become workout buddies. Because of him I get motivated to wake up an extra hour earlier so I can get in a run. Farhad may have talent, but he's still an aspiring actor. Teaching dancing classes just doesn't pay enough of his bills. Fortunately for him, he is also a skilled handy man, a skill he acquired working for his father's business as a kid down in Florida. For a minimal fee, he helps resurface the cabinets in the kitchen of my mom's house. He does such a good job that my mom refers him to all of her friends who need work done. "Thank you so much Auntie," Farhad easily charms people with his politeness and charm. "I really can't thank you enough for helping me out like this."

"Not a problem Beta," my mom says to him. "With me good work is always appreciated. But I think that you're charging much too little. Are you sure that you won't accept some more money."

"Auntie, please I can't. I feel bad enough taking money from Chhoto's mother as it is."

71

"Ok, then if you put it that way, then we're taking you out to dinner next week at Raga's, and no saying no. You can't say no to family."

The dinner at Raga's is great, and Ma also invites Shibi Mashi, Rana Da, and Seema. Basically, I think it's a treat for all those people who've helped Ma raise a bad kid like myself. Ma tells everybody how handy Farhad is with his tools, so when Seema and Rana Da mention that they want their kitchen tiles redone, I naturally help my new friend land yet another job.

Good friends. Loving family. A promising future. Life certainly feels much better now than when my father passed away. Things are meant to get better. We just need the help of our friends sometimes to keep things going forward.

Now I'm a college senior and I land a decent job lined up at a well-known consulting firm. And the firm's in midtown. Close to where my friends work, close to the number 7 and E trains that make the trip to my mom's house convenient and frequent. My friend Dave, now a senior at Tulane but scheduled to return to New York in the summer, and I consider getting a place together in midtown, only a few blocks away from Rana Da's apartment. Can things get any better than this? It's my final semester in college, and I'm trying not to slack off, but still, I can't seem to put in the same effort that I did for the past three and a half years. One Tuesday evening, I call up Rana Da. "Hey, what's up man," he says to me.

"Nothing. Just chilling. I got no classes tomorrow morning."

"Oh, cool, so why don't you swing by the Social, we'll have a couple of drinks."

It sounds good to me, so I walk up to Christopher Street and take the number 1 train up to 50th Street and make my way to the Social. Rana Da's there still dressed in his work suit, but with bloodshot eyes. I already see three empty bottles of Heineken in front of him. "Have a beer," he says.

I grab a Heineken bottle. "What's the occasion?"

"What do you mean?" he says, obviously drunk.

"What're you celebrating for?"

"Just happy to see family."

I smile and hold my bottle to his. "Cheers."

It's odd. For the next few nights, Rana Da always calls me from a bar. I have to decline every night as I got classes then, but on Friday, I'm able to make it over. He asks me to meet him at the Irish Pub. By the time I get there, he's already drunk. I see him approach a nice looking thin girl with reddish blonde hair. "Hey beautiful," he says to her. "Can I buy you a drink?"

She smiles at him, but before she can say anything, a blonde guy, semi-well built, approaches Rana Da and shoves him. "Yo, stay the fuck away from my girl." Rana Da pushes him back, and there would've been a fistfight within seconds had not the bouncer intervened. I rush over, and grab Rana Da, and say to the bouncer that I'll escort him out. The bouncer agrees while he restrains the jealous boyfriend. I pull Rana Da out onto Seventh Avenue.

"Yo, what the fuck are you doing!"

"What do you mean what the fuck am I doing!" He shouts in awkward drunkenness. "I was just having some fun."

"I think you're a little too drunk to be having fun. I don't get it man. How'd you become such a slave to the booze? You got it all. The job, the wife . . ."

"Not much longer," he says.

I stop and stare at him bewildered. Something just came out of left field. "What, are you getting fired?"

He shakes his head no.

"Are you getting divorced?"

He shakes his head yes.

"Yo Rana. Rana Da. Don't even fuck around with shit like that."

"I don't fuck around with shit like that."

"What the fuck happened. You two looked so happy together."

He loosens his tie and stares onto the busy street with the cars passing by. He's about to deliver a monologue. "You know how Seema miscarried a few months ago?" I shake my head, I did not know about this. If my mom knew, she did not mention it to me. He goes on. "Well, it was really an abortion. You see, we had an accident, and then she missed her period, and she said that she wasn't ready to be a mother yet. I was a bit excited about having a kid, but didn't oppose, because, after all, it was her body, but if she wasn't ready, then I couldn't push her. I mean, it is her body." I stand there in silence, listening to him. I don't say anything, but listen to what he has to say. "You see, Seema really enjoys being a social butterfly and going on photo shoots, and being noticed by people."

"Well, it should boost your ego, right?" I try to break the tension.

"To be honest," he loosens his tie, "it can get to be a nuisance after a while. Ok, then, it turns out that even though I was cool that she got the abortion and all, that wasn't enough. She wanted to be freer and to her marriage seemed more like a jail than anything. Then she met Farhad." He chokes, he looks ready to cry. I've never seen him this upset.

I don't know how to react. Here I am staring at the man who practically saved my life and I have to acknowledge that I am responsible for introducing to him the man who breaks up his marriage. "Rana Da, . . . oh shit, look, . . . I am so fucking sorry . . . I had no idea . . ." I drift away into an angry dream, where I'm beating Farhad to death, me pinning him against the concrete with my knees and then sending lethal blows to his head, crashing it against the pavement. He may be a nationally ranked athlete, but I learned to fight on the streets of

New York. My angry thoughts are interrupted when Rana Da places his hand on my shoulder. I'm not certain if it is to comfort me and assure me that all will be ok or to lean against me and support himself. "That's ok. You didn't make her cheat on me."

"But what now?"

He shrugs his shoulder. For the first time in my life, I see that he is clueless. That he doesn't have an answer. There is a bewildered look in his eyes, questioning what he did to deserve such ill treatment from a woman he loved. I've never ever seen him look vulnerable. Not ever before this. Yeah, I can no longer afford to indulge in wrath and have him calm me down. I realize that it is my duty to keep him away from bars and to assure him that he deserves better. I must now assume my role as the big brother and assure Rana that everything will be all right. I must now begin to watch over him.

-For Tadvana Narayanan
02.15.2005

My Name

When I was studying for the SATs, I memorized like a gazillion words, and then forgot most of them, except for the word iconoclastic. That's probably because I wished my parents could've shed some of the traditions they brought with them from Kolkata, like the no beef eating policy. Or I wish they could've at least used utensils when they at their food rather than feeding off their fingers and making as much noise as humanly possible at the dinner table. But if there was one tradition that I wished they could've forgotten about, it was the one about nicknames.

You see, my parents named me twice. Yes, just like in Jhumpa Lahri's *The Name Sake*. The first time, my parents named me Ajay, which was to be my good name, the one people at school and work would refer to me as, the one that would be labeled on my birth certificate and driver's license. Then, like most Bengali parents, they gave me a nickname, that everyone at home and the community was supposed to refer to me as. My problem was that my nickname became my good name, and it probably started with all the Bengali kids I grew up with calling me Baboo. You see, my Mom and I left Kolkata when I was five, to join my Dad, or as I call him, Baba, in New York, who was already there for three months. Baba was staying with his college friend, Asim Guha. Asim Kaku to me. And Asim Kaku had a son my age, Suvro, who immediately started to call me Baboo, since that's what he heard my parents and his parents call me.

Within a few weeks, Baba found us an apartment in Floral Park. And fortunately for me, when I enrolled in school, Suvro was in my Kindergarten class. But already being in the habit of calling me Baboo, that's what he called me in school. Soon, all the other kids, both the boys and girls, started to call me that. So did my teacher, Mrs. Wolfe. So, throughout junior high and even a little bit through high school, I was Baboo.

You want to know what the worst part of being known as Baboo was? Well, as a kid, I wasn't exactly what you'd call skinny. No, I was short and chubby, and not very well coordinated in sports. So, when I took extra time to finish a race, or when I couldn't make a basket, or when I couldn't catch a fly ball, do you know what I was called? Yup, you got it. The big dumb baboon!

So, my nickname Baboo stuck until the beginning of ninth grade, when my Dad told us that we'd be moving to LA because he just got a tenured teaching position at UC Riverside. It felt weird leaving the place I called home for the past nine years. Suvro's parents threw my family a surprise going away party. It felt really sad leaving all my friends and the routine I grew accustomed to, but hey, I did watch Beverly Hills 90210 a lot, so I figured I could make my fantasies a reality.

It wasn't too difficult to adjust to life in the West Coast. My family quickly made friends in the Bengali community there.

My parents at first began to introduce me to their new Bengali friends as Baboo, but I became determined to correct that from the start. "Look," I said to my parents one time at the dinner table. "I'm not a kid anymore."

My dad was still in the habit of licking the last bits and pieces of rice and vegetables off his fingers, and my Mom was already piling the dishes into the sink.

"You're not?" said my dad. "That's great, then you can start paying rent for your room. It could really help me out with the mortgage payments."

"That's not what I mean. Don't you think I'm a little too old for you still to be calling me Baboo?"

"How can you be too old for a name?" said my mom.

"Look, Baboo's a kiddie name."

"It's the name your grandfather gave you," said my mom. "Are you ashamed of what your grandfather wants?"

"No, it's just . . . fine, you can call me Baboo at home . . . but can I just be called Ajay outside?"

My parents decided that was fair, and so finally, I was called Ajay. I became involved in track and tennis, and no one any longer called me Baboo. After high school, I attended school at UCLA where I majored in computer engineering and economics. At UCLA, I had a great time, and tried to be an active member of the Indian student organizations there. Everyone there knew me as Ajay. Well, most of the time. One time, the Indian organization invited Swagota Banerji to attend a seminar. Yes, Swagota Banerji, the American Bengali soap opera actress who won an Emmy award for her portrayal of some Hispanic character. My parents knew her parents well back in the east coast, so when she appeared at UCLA, I approached her and asked her if she remembered me. "Give me a hint" she said, genuinely confused.

"Ajay," I tried to rekindle her memory. "Ajay Sinha. I grew up in Bellerose . . ."

"Oh, that's right," she finally remembered. "Baboo. How are you? How're your parents?"

From that incident, many of my friends began to ask me the deal about Baboo, but that name fortunately did not stick. After graduation, I landed a job with a media-technology company that required me to return to New York.

When I returned to New York via LaGuardia Airport, Asim Kaku waited for me at the passenger pickup terminal. Remembering how close our family was to his, the first thing I did was go and touch his feet, since my Mom told me to do that at least a dozen time before I departed LA. "Hey Baboo," he spoke to me in Bengali. "You've grown so tall and become so skinny." I had no idea that he was going to call me Baboo and throughout the car ride to his house, he constantly referred to me as that.

Asim Kaku's wife, Shefali Kaki had a nice warm meal of rice, lentil, and chicken waiting for me. "I remember how much you loved chicken, so I cooked more than enough of it, Baboo. Don't be shy. Eat as much as you want."

They asked me about my parents, and they asked me about life in California, and they told me that I always had a home here in good old Bellerose. Suvro would be back tomorrow night as he was touring Europe after graduating from Cornell and before starting his job as an Investment Banker. "You and Suvro could have found a place together in Manhattan," Shefali Kaki reminded me, but I told her that my company already helped me secure a subsidized studio in Chelsea.

I spent the night in Suvro's old bedroom, a place that I was quite familiar with as during elementary school, I spent several sleepovers here. Back then, Asim Kaku would bring in the television set to that room, and when we were supposed to be watching movies like *E.T.* or *The Alley Cats*, we in reality were watching *Friday the 13th* or *Nightmare of Elm Street*. Once, we got so freaked out with *Halloween*, that when we heard the bathroom door in the hallway open, we both shrieked and jumped and then we ended up knocking the lamp off the bedside table. The shattering glass caused Asim Kaku to come in and see what the matter was. When he found out that we were secretly watching horror films, he gave us both a painful scolding and he even yelled at me like I was his own son.

Suvro arrived early the next day, while I was still in the process of waking up as my mind was still in the West Coast time zone. Suvro had brought home with him some of his Cornell friends, a tall slender blonde guy named Terry, and a fair looking brown haired girl named Audrey. While Suvro introduced his friends to his parents, his mom pointed to me coming down the stairs, still dressed in my nightclothes, hair not combed, face not shaven. When I looked at Audrey, I wished I had gotten a warning. I would have at least slipped on a robe and tucked my hair into a baseball cap.

79

"Hey Baboo," Suvro says to me. He got up off his couch to give me a hug. "Welcome home. Meet my friends. This is Terry, and this is Audrey. This is Baboo. We practically grew up together. Until he moved out West."

"Nice to meet you," Audrey says. "You said your name is Baboo?"

"Actually, it's . . ."

"Yeah, it's Baboo," said Suvro. "We practically grew up in each other's houses. We used to watch horror movies together when we were really supposed to be watching cartoons. You know, he even broke my lamp once."

"No, no," I say, "That was you who broke the lamp." And I get so wrapped up in that friendly debate that I eventually realized that Audrey and Terry left to go home, thinking that my name was actually Baboo.

A week later, I moved into my studio, a place not quite the home I would have imagined. It was pretty tiny, but it didn't bother me much since I spent much of my time either at work, attending client meetings, business seminars, or parties in the City. My work was in Soho but I got to travel around the city quite a bit, selling the company's products and services. I became close friends with a few guys from work and we formed a regular clique and went to bars as often as possible. One Thursday night, we were drinking at the Limerick on 23rd Street when I heard someone call out, "Hey, isn't that Baboo." It was Audrey, she was hanging out with a few friends from Cornell.

"Audrey, hey what's up," I kissed her on her cheek hello. "What's going on? What're you doing here?"

"Oh, just a bunch of Cornell people getting together. Suvro should be here soon."

And sure enough, Suvro did make it. Someone familiar, someone I remembered from the Bengali community when I was growing up in Queens, accompanied him. "Baboo," Suvro says, "What're you doing here?"

"Just hanging out with some of my boys." I turned to his friend. "Say, man, you look familiar, what's your name."

His friend shook my hand saying, "Yeah, I remember you. My name's Ajay. Ajay Sen." Of course I remembered this kid. He was around my age, and sometime during fifth grade his parents moved to India for two years and came back to America to settle on Long Island. What I remember most about him was that he shared the same name as me, but he got to use his name while I didn't. "Your name's Ajay too, right?" I began to like the kid already.

"Yeah, you got a sharp memory. So, tell me, whatcha been up to lately."

He sat down on the stool next to me, and ordered a Heineken. Suvro, seemed relieved, and he went over to talk to Audrey. "Oh, I'm finishing up my degree at Baruch."

"Cool, that's right down the street."

"Yep."

"What're you majoring in?"

"I'm concentrating in Information Systems and Economics."

"Good stuff," I said, taking a sip of my martini. "I did something like that at UCLA. So, you looking for a job after graduation?"

"Nah," he shook his head with an impeccable confidence. "I'm gonna make it on my own. Getting ready to launch a business."

"Wow," I was truly impressed that a guy my age was already striking it out on his own. "That's really cool man. Hey, if you make it big, you can offer me a job."

"Sure," he says, "I can probably get you in now. I'll talk to some of my partners, and we should be able to get you in." He pulls out his wallet to hand me a business card. It was a really plain card, which had on it only his name, telephone, and e-mail. I gave him my own card, and on the back of it jotted down my cell phone number.

"Ok man, give me a ring some time," I said to him. "We can grab a beer and go see the Knicks or something."

"No doubt."

I got up to go talk to Suvro, and little did I know that Ajay Sen got up and trailed behind me too. Suvro was seated next to Audrey in a booth and they were each drinking out of a Budweiser can.

"Baboo," Suvro says to me, "Have a seat. Tell me what's been up with you. How does it feel to be back in the Big Apple?"

When I sat down, I grabbed some of the French fries off his plate. "Dude, why can't you call me by my real name?"

"Whatcha talking about?"

"You called me Baboo."

"Yeah, so what, I've been calling you Baboo since we could talk."

"Yeah, but we're not five anymore. That was a nickname, and I think I've grown out of it since then. I'd prefer to be called Ajay."

Suvro laughs and takes a sip of his drink. "Yo, I think that's too much to ask man. It's a habit that's too hard to break."

"I think that Baboo's a cute name," Audrey giggled and took a sip of her drink too. "And plus, isn't that other guy named Ajay too. It'll get confusing."

It was then that I realized that Ajay Sen was no longer sitting next to us. I looked around and noticed instead that he was making friends with Suvro's other friends, shaking their hands and introducing himself. "Yeah," I said, "That's right, but at least he addresses me by my real name."

"Ok man," Suvro finished his drink and raised his hands, like he was complying with something he was reluctant to do. "I'll try, but I can't be making no promises."

Sure enough, Ajay Sen called me the very next day. "Ajay, what's up. It's Ajay Sen."

I liked this kid better and better. "Hey, what's up man! What's going on?"

"Oh, just wanted to say that it was really great seeing you again after all these years."

"Yeah, same here. So, what's up? You wanna do something this weekend?"

"I'd like to," he said. "But I might have to work this weekend?"

"Work? On the weekends?"

"Yeah man, when you're building something from ground up, you need to dedicate pretty much all your time to it at first. Then you can retire like when you're thirty. Say man, do you like what you do?"

"I guess so," I walked around my small studio, and when I realized there was not enough room to explore, and began to walk on top of my couch, and then hopped on to my bed, and back and forth. "I mean, it's not my dream job if that's what you mean?"

"I hear you. You pretty much gotta make your dream job. Say, what're you doing this Saturday?"

"Don't know, don't got any solid plans yet. Why, you wanna do something?"

"Sure," he said. "After I'm free. But I'm holding a seminar for clients in Queens. Why don't you swing by then? It'll be a good way for you to meet my partners and I can probably get you in right away."

"Really, could you do that?" I was intrigued. This kid was at most a year younger than me and he was already in the process of building a business and talking to partners to expand his equity.

"Yeah, why not. I can put in a good word for you and coming from me you'll look really good."

So that following Saturday I took the Q train to Times Square and then jumped on to number 7 train that took me into Long Island City. I followed Ajay Sen's instructions, which led me to a glass corporate building right across the street from the Citigroup tower. I went into the lobby where an old man wearing a security uniform who looked Indian, sat behind the lobby counter. "What can I do for you?"

"Oh hey, I'm here to see Ajay Sen?"

The security guard stared at me, all perplexed.

"It's something about a meeting for his startup firm?"

The security guard pulled out a blue binder, which must have been his schedule book. "All we got right now, is a meeting for QuickFix, and that's down at the basement. Maybe that's what you're talking about?"

"Could be, he didn't tell me that name of his company, he just said that's it's in this building at this time."

"Then it's QuickFix. Take the first elevator bank down to the basement and make your first right."

"Thanks."

The security guard was right, because in one of the rooms at the basement I saw people in the process of arranging folding chairs in neat rows of two aisles right in front of a huge projection screen. Ajay Sen stood near the entrance, dressed in a black suit. Looking at him, you could tell that he just got his hair cut and his shoes polished today. The minute he saw me, he walked all the way over from the center podium and shook my hand. "Hey, man, it's great that you could make it.

"Yeah, sure," I said. "You got my interest."

"Why don't you sit up there in the front? I'll introduce you to my partners when we're done with the film."

"You guys did a film?"

"Yeah, about the company. Image is important to us."

I sat at the front, and turned my head to gradually notice all sorts of people come in dressed in a variety of wardrobes from three-piece suits to simply tshirts and jeans. Gradually, they dimmed the lights and a tall portly gentleman walked to the middle of the podium dressed in slacks, a black t-shirt, and a sports coat. "Good Evening," he said. "My name's Aaron McLeod, and I'm the regional head of QuikFix. Thanks for coming in tonight. If you stick around, you'll come to see that if this is for you, then in a short period of time you could be ready to retire. That was my case. I actually didn't go to college. Instead, after high school, I worked in construction until someone, I met at a party, introduced me to QuickFix. Then, like you I was sitting in the audience. I left my cushion of a gig in the family business, and I took a chance with this. And because I did, now I have more money than I ever possibly could've made in construction. The same could happen to you, with just some hard work. This isn't for everybody, but I'll take you as long as you fit one requirement. That you stay hungry and eager to succeed."

He then went on to show a video that demonstrated the workings of QuickFix, about how one joins the company, and then recruits more manpower to help sell their products and services, and the more people one recruits, the better a chance he or she had to succeed. Oh, God, I just realized that this company worked on a pyramid scheme. I turned around, and in the dark I noticed some people intrigued, while others were as disappointed as I was. Some of them actually got up and walked out during the middle of the film. I stuck around because I figured I'd give Ajay the courtesy of letting him know that I was not interested. That twenty-minute video felt like it lasted for three hours. And then Aaron McLeod stood and spoke for another ten minutes about how he was a self-made millionaire and that if anyone was as diligent as he was, they could be as well. Finally, he concluded his remarks and I felt a need to breathe a sigh of relief. I went over to Ajay Sen who said, "Well, what ya think?"

"It's ok," I lied. "Not bad, but it's not for me."

"What, how could you say that when you haven't even seen what else is ahead?"

I wanted to say, "I've seen enough", but instead, I said, "Ok, but I'm gonna be busy for like the next couple of weeks with work and all."

"So, you can't make the meeting this coming Tuesday."

"Absolutely not! Maybe next time. Anyway, I got to hop. I've got to meet some friends in midtown."

As I rode up the elevator, one kid, who looked about my age, dressed in a suit said, "No way I'm coming to that again. It's like one of those get rich quick ads you see early Saturday mornings."

I laughed, and then headed for the number 7 train, to take me back to Manhattan.

That same week I changed my cell phone number for two reasons. One, my contract with my carrier was over, and I wanted a better service. The second was that since I now lived in New York, I figured I would keep a New York number. Things at work were not going very well, as my company started to do very poorly in sales. Our CEO had a meeting with all of us and said that though we were all guaranteed to be on the payroll for the next six months, there would be no guarantee of employment after that, and that it would be wise for all of us to start seeking work outside the company. Nice guy. He tried his best not to cry when he told us that the company he built from scratch was near collapse. He gave each of us a manila folder, which included a list of preferred headhunters, all of whom he had personal relationships with.

Within the middle of the week, one headhunter set me up with an interview at an investment bank. The name of the bank seemed very familiar. Of course, it was the same place where my childhood friend Suvro worked. Perhaps he could offer me some tips to prepare.

I called Suvro up a few times, but it went directly to his voicemail. I left him messages saying, "Suvro, what's up, it's Ajay, please call me back." Two days went by and I never got a call from him. I figured that he must've been busy with his job and all. I tried him again, that Friday. This time, he did pick up.

"Hello?"

"Suvro?"

"Yeah, who's this?"

"It's Ajay man."

"Ajay," he spoke rather curtly, and quickly. "I can't hear you. I'm in a bar. It's really loud. I'm going to have to call you back later when I get better reception." He hung up quickly.

That felt really weird. Why would Suvro not want to talk to me? I've known him all my life. And he seemed to hear me well when he answered the phone. So why did he make up stuff about there being bad reception and all? Not a very good liar, was he? During my few seconds of contemplation, my cell phone rings again. It's Suvro's number. "Suvro, what's the deal, can you hear me now."

"Dude," he said, this time much more friendly. "I call you Baboo for a reason."

"Huh? What, you mean old habits die hard?"

"That and if you must go by Ajay, then whenever you call, you'll have to mention your full name."

"Why?"

"Because Ajay Sen keeps calling me about this pyramid scheme and he just won't leave me alone about it."

I started to laugh, and realized that I did not give Ajay Sen my updated cell phone number. "Fine," I said to him, "Then Baboo it is. So listen, I have an interview coming up with your firm."

"Yeah, when?"

"Sometime next week."

"Ok, once you get the names, let me know. I'll put in the good word Baboo."

Perhaps being called Baboo would have its benefits after all. It was nice to have friends, especially childhood friends. And what better way to be reminded of that than a childhood nickname.

-For Arnab Das
8.9.2005

The White Sari

"What's wrong Sandhya Di?" Pradeep, walked into the living room where she was seated on the couch still wearing the red sari she had left home wearing in the morning. She sat on the couch watching a video of Satyajit Ray's film Apur Shanshar. Very few families still had VCRs in their homes nowadays, but a few weeks after Sandhya came to work in this house to help care for Pradeep's young son, Pradeep had ordered one for her online. Many of the old Bengali films she enjoyed were yet to be released on DVD. Every few weeks, Pradeep would return home from work, with another film for Sandhya Di.

"Nothing," she responded.

"Then are you just watching a sad film?" he laughed and sat down on his armchair sitting directly across from her. She had this upset look on her face ever since this afternoon when she returned home from Bhakti Majumdar's house in Queens. "Come on, what is it? Is it some bad news from home?"

Home, was Bagura, a town in Bangladesh, where her son still lived in his grandfather's ancestral home and still worked at his late father's jewelry shop. But with the influx of more established commercial competitors, the business lately experienced an exodus of what was known as rather loyal customers. With simply a high school education and a dearth of capital to invest in proper training, her son, Goutam was at a loss to succeed. So when she finally won the lottery to come to America, she decided that she would work hard and sponsor her son to come here. Just like a Bengali woman, about whom she had heard of living in Boston, had done years before. That woman eventually brought her son, who initially worked as a cab driver, then a mechanic, and finally opened his own garage. Such an American dream was not imaginable back home.

"No, no trouble at home," she said.

Pradeep had offered to lend her money before, in addition to her salary, so she could send it to her son to invest in business. He said she could pay back whenever, but had never inquired about when she would return it. He relished the meals that Sandhya would cook for his family and though he did not conceal his preference for her rui fish, he never made any demands. Just occasional requests and suggestions! But never demands! Whatever meal she prepared he and his family ate. One of her first Sunday nights, his wife Mona asked her to make some delicious chicken chops, which she had prepared for the Durga festival, but Pradeep interfered, "No, it's Sunday night and she's not working. If you're craving the food, go to Oak Tree road and buy some yourself."

Such incidents occurred often during Sandhya Di's first few weeks. Pradeep spent much of his time correcting Mona's trifle demands. "What's this?" Pradeep said to Mona one day, when he noticed that she set aside a cheap silver colored steel plate and glass on the kitchen table.

"That's for Sandhya Di so she could have dinner."

"Sandhya Di will eat in the same plates and glasses that we do! And she'll eat with us."

Eventually Mona's bickering and petty demands came to an end when she realized that her husband would tolerate none of them. Pradeep told their young son Bobby that he must treat Sandhya as his aunt, address her as Mashi, and listen to everything she had to say. "Sandhya Mashi is here to help take care of you. She cooks your favorite food for you. If she weren't here, you'd have to stay in after-school care. So be nice to her." Pradeep dictated this rule from the very beginning of Sandhya's tenure there, so his wife's influence on their son towards her could be minimal, if not negligible.

"Sandhya Di," Pradeep said. "Bobby came to me and said 'Sandhya Mashi looks sad today Baba.' And because you're sad, he's sad. Is everything ok?"

"Bhakti Boudi yelled at me today," Sandhya Di said.

By Bhakti Boudi, Pradeep knew that she meant Bhakti Majumdar. Yes, he knew of her well. So immense was her reputation that he heard of her within his first week of immigrating to New York from India. Besides running a successful dermatology practice located on Flushing's Parson's Boulevard, she remained very active in the Bengali community, serving on many committees dedicated to preserving and cultivating the Bengali culture in America. Her husband, Prabhanghsu Majumdar pioneered this movement in the mid sixties in New York's upper west side, but she made it flourish. Of what little Pradeep knew of Bhakti Majumdar, he found her to be direct, yet honest and upfront.

Pradeep still remembered the time when he started attending Durga Puja at some high school in Queens when first migrating to America. Bhakti Majumdar's husband helped the priest prepare for the Puja. When the priest dropped a wooden stick to be used for the Puja on the ground, Bhakti Majumdar's husband, Prabhangshu, offered to pick it up. But before he could reach the stick, the priest screamed out, "Hey hey! Don't touch that! It's only for Brahmins."

When she heard this insult to her husband, Bhakti Majumdar stopped with her own decorations and said, "What do you mean only Brahmins can touch that? When you needed my husband to sponsor you for work, where were your Brahmin friends? If you're gonna act like that, go back to whatever village you come from."

Bhakti Majumdar couldn't have been older than Sandhya Di, and Pradeep even guessed that Bhakti Majumdar was at least five years younger. So Pradeep did find it awkward when Sandhya Di addressed Bhakti Majumdar as Boudi, a Bengali salutation reserved for someone significantly older. But since Bhakti

Majumdar didn't seem bothered by it, he didn't give it much thought.

Others did not react to such shenanigans so lightly. A few weeks ago, Pradeep had been invited to the house of one of the traders at his former bank, Rana, who also happened to be Bengali. Rana's mother Shivani was present there, and Sandhya Di addressed Rana's mom as Mashima, a Bengali term for Auntie, reserved for the equivalent of a Mother's sister. Shivani, herself obviously younger than Sandhya Di retorted, "Why're you calling me Mashima for! I'm not old enough to be your Mashima, you'd be my Mashima if anything." Pradeep had interfered in time and told Shivani, "It was a mistake. She probably did it because I called you Mashima." But Bhakti Majumdar never seemed so irascible to such incidents.

"What happened at Bhakti Majumdar's?" He knew that Sandhya Di's brother-in-law had flown in from Dallas to New York two days ago and was scheduled to fly back today via JFK airport and Sandhya Di wanted to see him. Pradeep himself could only drive up to Manhattan. And a friend of Sandhya Di's from Brooklyn, Naeem Saeed, had volunteered to escort her from Manhattan to the Majumdar residence in Fresh Meadows in his own cab so she could meet with her brother-in-law.

"She yelled at me for not wearing a white sari!"

"What!"

"Yes, she yelled at me, saying that my husband died years ago, and that I should follow tradition and only wear white saris." Sandhya Di was on the verge of crying, and she pulled out a handkerchief concealed in the girdle underneath her sari. She didn't wail out loud, but she did lift her glasses slightly to wipe her eyes.

Pradeep noticed his son Bobby standing in the entrance to the family room, staring at his nanny, wondering why she was upset. "Bobby, can you go upstairs and watch some TV. Sandhya Mashi needs some privacy." The boy hesitated, but then heeded his father's request.

"She really scolded you for not following tradition?"

"Yes," Sandhya Di almost choked on her own sobbing. "She said that, and she said it in front of everyone. I've never been so insulted in my life."

Pradeep rested his head against his armchair. Tradition? According to her reputation Bhakti Majumdar was born Bhakti Chatterjee, to a prominent family that migrated from Barisal, Bangladesh to Kolkata. She earned the wrath of her Brahmin family when she opted to marry a fiancé coming from the very lowest caste, an act that back then would most certainly be considered rebellious rather than progressive. Her husband's last name was the same as Sandhya Di's, but they were not related. Bhakti Majumdar's eldest son, a medical school dropout, lived in Manhattan with his semi-professional model girlfriend. And there was no hint of them being even engaged. All this, and Bhakti Majumdar gave a poor old woman flak for the clothes she wore? "Don't worry Sandhya Di, Bhakti Majumdar will get a piece of my mind."

The main reason he wanted someone like Sandhya Di caring for his home and family was because like him, she was Bengali, and his biggest fear was that Bobby would grow up in Edison without learning to speak it. And to add to the treat, she excelled at cooking and she compulsively cleaned the house. Thanks to Sandhya Di, Pradeep lived in a spotless house. Alice from the Brady Bunch could not have kept the Brady home in better order.

Pradeep's wife Mona had a tinge of the Veronica syndrome, but she had married no Archie who'd comply to her idiosyncrasies. If Pradeep would be an Archie, it'd be Archie Bunker, not Archie Andrews. Unlike Bhakti Majumdar's husband, he wore the pants in his family. Bhakti Majumdar wielded such a strong influence on her family that Prabhanghsu Majumdar may as well have changed his name to Prabhansghu Chatterjee when he married his wife.

But no one was going to push Pradeep around into treating other people disparagingly. Not even his wife, the military brat who got tutored at the best prep schools throughout India, and who could boast a Western upbringing, even if she had been raised in the Eastern part of the world. She may have been raised in royalty, but Mona had not married into royalty. If she wanted the princess stature, she'd have to work for it again, from ground up.

Mona was not a bad person, just a bit snotty. But Pradeep had been able to mold her, and he did it without beating her the way Carlo Rizzi did Don Corleone's daughter in Mario Puzo's *The Godfather*. No, he loved his wife, and through tough love, he taught her subtly to respect other people, and to denounce her belief in the caste system. Within the first few weeks, Mona herself began to address Sandhya as Sandhya Di, and spoke to her directly. She would come home, and even inquire about Sandhya Di's well being as well as that of her son in Bagura and her sister in Dallas. One could argue that Mona's abrupt niceness spawned from fear of her husband's rage, but Pradeep sincerely believed that he had shown Mona the proper way to treat another human being. She had come to accept Sandhya Di as part of her family. Yes, Sandhya Di was family. She cared for his son, and she kept his house in order. She made sure that he always came home to a savory Bengali meal after a tough day at work, only exacerbated by the commute back to New Jersey. What right did someone else have to insult and criticize a member of his family?

Pradeep lay awake at night while Mona was already in a deep slumber, her arm thrown over his torso in abandon. Bhakti Majumdar may have been on the board for the New York Children's Hospital, she may have been the chair of Elliot Spitzer's public relations

committee, and she may have influence over some
Columbia Medical School admissions officer, but none
of that rationalized they way she spoke to a member of
his family. He glanced at the digital Bose alarm clock
resting on his bedside table. Four thirty in the morning.
Still too early to call, and sometime within the next three
hours Bobby would escape his own room and infiltrate
the master bedroom, agilely entering without the door
making a sound. Then he'd deftly make his way
between himself and Mona.

Later, while Bobby and Mona still slept in
during the Saturday morning, as did Sandhya Di,
Pradeep made his way downstairs to the kitchen. It was
nine o'clock and he flipped on the small TV, adjusting it
from the Cartoon Network to CNN. It just occurred to
him then that his former colleague Rana knew the
Majumdar family well. The Majumdar family helped
raise Rana in New York after his father had walked out
on him. Grabbing his cell phone, Pradeep dialed Rana.

"Hello, Rana, this is Pradeep."

"Oh, hey, what's up man!"

"Nothing much, I didn't wake you, did I?"

"No, not at all. I'm at the gym."

"Oh, ok. Let me ask you something? Are you
still in touch with the Majumdar family? Prabhangshu
and Bhakti Majumdar."

"Sure, my mom talks to Prabhanghsu Mesho and
Bhakti Mashi all the time. I still hang with the older son
Neil from time to time. Why? What's up?"

"How are they as people? Are they nice
people?"

"Yo, they're like one of the closest people I got
to family. I mean, when my dad walked out on us, they
gave me and my mom a lot of support. They even
helped me out a bit when I was going through my
divorce."

"So you don't think that they'd ever
intentionally hurt anyone right."

"Yo, I know they never would. They're one of the most selfless people I know. Why, what's going on?"

"Well, you see, my son's sitter . . ."

"Oh, you mean the one who's like ten years older than my mom but called her Mashi," Rana laughed into the receiver.

"Yeah! Her! Well she went to their house yesterday, and something happened."

"What? Did she call some twenty year old girl Dida?" Dida was a term reserved for a grandmother or a grandmother like figure.

Pradeep returned the laugh. "I don't know, but something happened, and I'm not sure what. Can you try to find out?"

"I'll try, but no promises." The call ended, and Pradeep spent the rest of the weekend like he normally did. He took his son to the courts trying to teach him to play tennis. He went to Oak tree road with Mona and he purchased items off of Sandhya Di's shopping list. And then he ended the day by watching 60 minutes and subsequently the Simpsons with his son.

Rana did not return his call. Not until Tuesday. "Pradeep, it's Rana."

"Hey Rana."

"Ok, I found out some things for you. First tell me this, did your nanny go to their place on Friday?"

"Yes, to meet her brother-in-law."

"Before he left to go to the airport, right?"

"Yes."

"And some guys Naeem and Mohammed Saeed drove her there from the city?"

"Yes, that sounds right."

"Ok, I'm not sure what you heard from your nanny, but listen to the version I heard."

On a Friday afternoon, Bhakti Majumdar had to leave the chamber rather quickly. Dilip Hazra had called early in the morning and said that he'd be stopping by at the last minute before he left for the airport. His sister-in-law called shortly afterwards. "Bhakti Boudi, how are you. I'm calling from Edison." Sandhya Di never identified herself by her own name. Instead, she would say where she was calling from, or better yet, where she lived.

"Yes, how are you?"

"My brother-in-law is coming to your house?"

"Yes he is."

"Can I come too?"

"Yeah, of course."

"Can you pick me up?"

"No, there's no way I can make it to New Jersey and back in time. Not today. Do you think that Pradeep can drop you off at the E train near the Port Authority and then you can get to Continental and I'll have one of my sons pick you up from there?"

Sandhya Di hesitated a bit before she answered. "Uh, travel alone on the bus?"

"No, the train. It's an easy ride."

"Let me call you back."

Ten minutes later Sandhya Di called back. "Boudi, Pradeep is driving into work today and he'll drop me off at Manhattan. Do you know Naeem Saeed?"

"Yeah, I think my husband might know him. Does he own a grocery store in Brooklyn?"

"Yes, that's him. His brother drives a cab and they said that they'll drive me from Manhattan to your house."

"Oh, ok, that's nice of them. I'll see you this afternoon then."

So, Bhakti Majumdar had to leave her chamber early, and leave the duties of the practice to her young associate dermatologist. She drove her Toyota Avalon down Northern Boulevard to Jackson Heights, to a store that sold Halal meat. Naeem and his brother would more than likely have a preference for such type of meat, whether or not they were devout Muslims. The gentleman behind the counter, Azim, recognized her immediately. "Bhakti Di, was my fish so good that have you come here to buy some more already?"

"Not today Azim Bhai. We got some unexpected company, and need some Hallal meat."

After Azim bagged the meat for her, he said, "Please give my regards to Prabhangshu Da."

Bhakti made it home quickly and started cooking the meat. Meanwhile, she readied the rice cooker and prepared a spinach dish. Her husband had already gone to pick up Dilip Hazra from the Continental Stop in Forest Hills. Sandhya Di and the Saeeds beat her husband and Dilip Hazra home. Mohammed Saeed parked the car near the curve while Naeem Saeed helped carry a large duffle bag that belonged to Sandhya Di into the house.

Bhakti stood confused. What was the duffle bag for? Did Sandhya Di intend to spend the night here at her house? If so, that was not a problem, but she would've preferred that she asked.

Sandhya Di, not necessarily as bucolic as she appeared, saw the look on Bhakti Majumdar's face and said, " these are just a few things that I am sending home with Dilip."

"Tell your brother to come in," Bhakti said to Naeem. "Two of you relax in the family room. Watch some TV, my husband and Dilip should be home soon."

"Thank you Didi," Naeem said. "Where is your restroom?"

"Down the hall, last door to your left. By the way, would you like milk and sugar in your tea?"

"Tea?" Naeem seemed unusually surprised.

"Yes, tea. You can't come to a Bengali home and not have tea."

"Ok, I'll have milk and sugar."

"And the same for your brother?"

"No, no sugar for him. His sugar is already too high."

"Ok."

"Boudi, can I help you?" Sandhya Di followed Bhakti Majumdar into the kitchen.

"Yes, please, the cups are in the cabinet right next to the fridge. If you could get the tea done, it'd be a great help."

Bhakti checked up on the meat, which looked like it was coming along fine. The rice was done, and she could relax a bit before serving the meal and setting the table. Sandhya Di already had the tea complete. Like a skilled samurai she prepared the tray well. But something looked odd. There were four matching mugs, and two plastic cups on the tray. Funny, she could've sworn that her husband had emptied the entire dishwasher last night. Oh man, he was getting older and more forgetful by the day. Just last week, an old friend of her son's called and when her husband answered the phone, the caller said, "Hi, is Niladri there?" He replied "Who?" For so many years they simply addressed their older son as Neil that he practically forgot their firstborn's proper name was Niladri.

"Don't we have enough mugs in the cabinet?" Bhakti walked over to the cabinet, opening it, and felt reassured that her husband's memory was not in such a dire need for immediate attention. "We have enough mugs."

"I know," said Sandhya Di. "We just don't feed them in regular cups?"

"Who?" Bhakti stood in her own kitchen, the same kitchen she'd owned and cooked in for the past twenty years, but right now she was so bemused, she could have been Alice in Wonderland.

Sandhya Di took a step closer towards Bhakti Majumdar, and whispered, "the Muslims."

Bhakti stared into her family room, and watched the two men, the two brothers. They sat cordially on the couch, and had not turned on the television. Mohammed rested his head against the couch, his eyes closed, while Naeem read the latest edition of the Bengali newspaper that her husband subscribed to and left on the coffee table. These two Muslim brothers took time out of their day and traveled out of their way to help an alleged friend travel from one borough to another because Sandhya Di felt too timid to ride the New York public transportation system.

Bhakti took the two plastic cups off the tray and hurled them into the sink. Had her younger son been there, he would've yelled, "Three pointer! Go Mom." But there was nothing there to break the tension. "Don't ever pull this shit off at my house ever again. They'll drink in the same cups that we do."

"But that's the tradition," Sandhya Di mumbled.

"What kind of fucked up bullshit tradition is this?" Yes, her rage in Bengali really coupled the English swear words, words that her younger son had begun using more liberally and frequently ever since becoming a portfolio manager at a new asset management fund in Westchester. "If you want to talk tradition then why aren't you wearing a white sari?"

"A white sari?" Sandhya Di stood there confused, and intimidated, like an innocent grocery store owner who had no idea why she needed to pay the local mafia chief protection money.

"Yeah a white sari! Don't play stupid with me. You know damn well what I'm talking about. Your husband died years ago."

"Yeah, so?"

"Then how come you're not wearing a white sari? Instead of following tradition, you go on all these shopping sprees in Jackson Heights and Oak Tree dressing like Rainbowbrite! Widows were also supposed to jump into their husband's funeral pyre in olden days. Are you for that tradition as well?"

Sandhya Di could take no more. Like a warrior being attacked by a volley of weapons on the battlefields of Kurukshetra, she knew that to overcome this enemy she'd have to use a superior weapon, one to deflect the incessant flow of these ordinary weapons. "Boudi," she stood up like a true warrior, ready to surprise her assailants who had foolishly underestimated her. "Read up on your history. Ram Mohan Ray stopped that disgraceful thing years ago."

"If you want to cite history," said Bhakti, "then you should keep up with current events too! America and India are both secular states where you don't discriminate people based on their religions."

Ouch, Sandhya Di again cringed back in fear. When Uncle Phil bailed out Will Smith from the Pool Hall in one episode of Fresh Prince, having his own cue stick would be no good if he didn't know how to shoot. She had remembered reading in the Ramayana and Mahabharata that simply knowing the mantra to a divine weapon was not enough. You had to learn everything about the weapon; otherwise, if you used it, you'd get destroyed. Just like the villain Ashwattaman who received tutelage about the Brahmaastra from his father Drona, but used it against superior warriors without mastering the use of it. Consequently, he got cursed to roam the Earth for three thousand years alone and without friends. "We were taught that the Muslims are inferior people," she said timidly to Bhakti Majumdar.

"My grandmother also taught me not to mix with people who weren't Brahmins," Bhakti said. "I loved her with all my life, but if I listened to everything she said, then I would've missed out on marrying the best guy in the world and two of the best sons. If you keep up with this shit, you might lose some of the best friends you make. How many people would take time out of their day to drive you around? Don't you dare ever pull this shit off again! Not in my house. Or else you'll never be welcome here."

Bhakti Majumdar then stormed to the cabinet, and got two matching mugs from the cupboard, poured the tea, served it herself, and then went off to set the table. She did all of those by herself, and only requested help when her husband finally did return with Dilip Hazra.

Pradeep sat at his desk as Rana relayed this story to him. "Ok Rana, thanks for letting me know."

"Not a problem, and if you're ever looking to make a move, let me know."

Pradeep got up and made his way to the men's room. He splashed water in his face and stared into the mirror. He knew that when he went home tonight, after dinner, he was going to have to have a talk with Sandhya Di. The same type of talk that he had with Mona not too long ago!

-For Ranajit Datta
05.21.2007

Accepted

"What's this?" Sam walked into the kitchen, after rushing down the stairs. It always took him longer to shower on weekends, a luxury he denied himself during the working days of the week. He prided himself on getting to work early. If you asked him, early meant getting in before seven in the morning! The way he was overstressed about his job, one would think he held a doctoral in medicine, not computer science.

"What's what?" Rina lifted her head from the weekend New York Times, taking a sip of her Darjeeling tea. She grabbed the remote off the round glass dinner table, and aimed it at the plasma screen television in the living room, shutting off CNN. Sanjay Gupta disappeared into the three basic colors.

Sam spun his keys around in a loop. His sneakers were already on. She gave up, after asking him time and again, not to wear outdoor footwear past the corridor of the front door. "You said you'd be ready."

"Yeah, and I am."

"No, you're not!"

"Yeah! I am!"

"Look Honey. Do you honestly plan on wearing your salwar kamiz to the picnic?"

"Uhm, yeah! Why?"

"Come on," he laughed. He laughed like a good sport who just realized he was duped on April Fools. "You can't do that!"

"What do you mean I can't do that?" She had stared at herself in the mirror before putting on this outfit, and she looked good. She knew it. She exercised regularly, running three miles every other day. It was Sam, on the other hand, who should be embarrassed with his clothes. He needed a new shirt, one at least one size larger. His disgusting large stomach made its presence known in his white polo that sported his company's logo.

"Come on Honey. There are going to be Americans here."

"Uhm, yeah," Rina took another sip of her tea. "That's the whole point of living in America."

"Look, seriously," Sam stopped swinging his keys and put them into his jean pocket. "It's not funny anymore."

"Who's laughing?"

"Rina! Will you stop it!"

"It's not like this is a beach party," she snapped back. "Look how cold it is. We're going to be inside. It's not like we're going to be playing beach volleyball. Or jumping into the pool."

He frowned, glaring at her through his thick lenses. "Damnit Rina. Why're you doing this to me? My boss is hosting this party!"

"And?"

"Look, this is getting ridiculous. Are you gonna change or not?"

"No Samir" she yelled at him. He never said that he hated being called by his full name, but he always addressed himself as Sam. "If you can't put up with having an Indian wife then maybe you should've told your mother to put an ad in white wash me dot com. Not Bharat Matrimony!"

Samir glared down at her. He looked ready to charge at her. But he was too out of shape and she was too quick for him. And anyway, she had taken some self-defense classes offered at her company gym, conducted by someone who was instructed by a direct disciple of Bruce Lee. She could take care of herself. "Look" Samir breathed heavily as he spoke. "You either go up and change or I'm going alone."

She barely waited for him to complete his sentence. "Have fun." She waived her hand at him. Then she grabbed the remote, turning the television back on.

He turned around and violently closed the front door behind him. The instant she heard his Mercedes back out of the driveway, she rose from her chair and made her way upstairs. She entered the master bedroom and grabbed some tear away Adidas pants and an MIT sweatshirt out of the armory. Ever since the miscarriage she experienced almost seven months ago, she no longer slept in this bedroom, but in the guestroom down the hall. Changing, she went back downstairs, grabbed some yogurt out of the fridge, and made herself comfortable on the couch. The television was still on and she flipped the channel from CNN to the local channel. The Red Sox were playing the Yankees. The Yankees! She changed immediately until she came to a re-run of Growing Pains. She really didn't watch television, but liked to keep it on. It made her feel like she had company.

When she moved from New Jersey to Boston to attend business school at Sloan, she honestly thought that she'd be in Boston for at most two years. But right before she started classes, her parents introduced her to Samir Pathak. They had heard about him through an Internet matchmaking site tailored towards Indians in America. In the eyes of her parents, Samir was perfect. The son of Brahmin parents, his family came from her home state of Maharashtra, and he graduated from Cornell, and completed his doctorate in computer science from Boston College. And he certainly wasn't some red headed Irish kid called Danny whom she never brought home but rather shamelessly fondled in public, sometimes in the presence of other Indians, who happened to be friends or acquaintances of her parents.

At the insistence of her parents, she met up with Samir in Boston a few weeks before she started classes when she came up to finalize her housing arrangements. They met at a coffee shop in Harvard Square.

"Rina?" He got up from a stool and walked up to her a few moments after she entered the front door. Back then, he did not have as large a stomach and he

105

looked like if he exercised, he could've been in better shape. Like Danny.

"Yeah."

"Hi," he smiled at her. "I'm Sam. How about that booth over there?"

"Ok."

He ordered two glazed donuts and a hot chocolate while she just stuck to a skim milk latte.

"So, when did you come here?" he asked.

"This morning."

He smiled, shaking his head. "No, I meant America. When did you come to this country?"

"Oh," she laughed. "Just before eleventh grade. Were you born here?"

"I was actually born in Calcutta. I moved to England when I was two, and came here when I turned five."

"Calcutta?" Did her parents look at the wrong profile on that website? She didn't think he was Bengali. Like Sunil, Danny's best friend, who was Bengali.

"Isn't your family Marathi?"

"Yeah, we are, but my grandparents moved there for business back in the day and my family's been there ever since."

He seemed nice enough then, and her parents called her immediately asking how it went. She said he seemed nice, which elated them. They encouraged her to meet him more.

"What do you think of him?" her father called her up that same very night.

"He's nice, I guess."

"Look, Lulu," her father called her by her childhood pet name. It was funny how her dad began to sound like the Sultan talking to Jasmine in Aladdin. "You're not getting any younger. It's important for you to find someone . . ."

"Bapu . . ."

"Look, I know you had your thing with that American boy. But you're getting older now. It's time you stop playing games and settle down. Like your sister."

"Bapu, I wasn't playing games."

"Lulu, it's important to preserve your culture. So you don't forget where we come from. Now you're saying that this Samir boy is nice?"

"Yeah, he seems nice."

"So give him more chances. For your mother! And me."

By the middle of her first semester at business school, her parents and Samir's parents proposed a wedding date, which was to happen during winter break. Samir's grandfather, a man of eighty-eight about to return to India, expressed fears that he wouldn't live long enough to return and see at least one of his grandchildren wed.

The ceremony was rather small, with only immediate family attending. In fact, her only guest other than her parents was her sister and her family, including a three-year-old nephew from Philadelphia. Sam's only guest other than his family was Kevin, another computer dweeb from Boston College. As soon as Sam finished his small lame speech, Kevin yelled out, "You're supposed to kiss the bride after the speech Sam."

"She doesn't know that," Sam said.

Many times right after college she wondered how Danny would kiss her at their wedding reception and their friends would applaud as Faith Hill's "The Way You Love Me" play in the background. But Sam's mother did not find such a song appropriate for a wedding. She wouldn't accept it.

Rina must've dozed off on the couch. The ringing of the phone awoke her. The television was still on. This probably explained why she dreamt about being back at the Hill Center at Rutgers. Endora, the mother from Bewitched was her instructor, listening

107

incredulously to Darren try to come up with an excuse for not submitting his numerical analysis homework. Weird, but dreams never made sense. She glanced at the caller ID. It was Samir's mother. Rina ignored it. All that woman would do was go on and on and tell her it was time for them to try to get pregnant again. The woman never knew when to shut up, raving on about her daughter and son-in-law making the big bucks with their law and medical practices. Last time Samir was away on a business trip, his mother called talking about how Samir's sister was lecturing at Harvard Law School, when, Rina knew that in reality Samir's sister only attended a seminar that happened to be hosted at Harvard. Rina had dozed off during that conversation, and when she awoke, Samir's mother was still talking, but this time about her son-in-law's new patent in cardiology research.

Bewitched came to an end and Archie's Weird Mysteries came on next. Archie. The redheaded Archie. She hadn't seen an Archie show on television for a long time. Then she realized why she always flipped past the Yankee games. Danny was a hard-core Yankee fan. He took her to Yankees Stadium many times and taught her about baseball. For his first birthday that they were together, she bought him a Don Mattingly autographed plaque.

Not a day passed by that she did not think about Danny, her college sweetheart and first love. Forget her first love. Her only love! Why did her father make her break up with him? Why was he so adamant and set in his ways?

She sighed. At last, her father was not to blame. The fault was hers. In their three years together, she never mentioned Danny to her parents. Not once. She never introduced them, and if she went away one weekend with Danny to Cooperstown or Atlantic City, she would simply tell her parents that she was going away with college friends. And that wasn't a lie. Just not the complete truth!

What was Danny up to? Was he married? Danny always wanted a big family.

To get her mind off Danny, she turned on her IBM ThinkPad to check her work e-mails. She worked as a product manager for a company that provided proprietary data to financial institutions, and recently she got promoted with the extra responsibility of handling the on-boarding of new clients. She surfed through the excel spreadsheet that her summer college intern, Elise, had prepared for her. Rina saw a new client name, which she didn't recognize, some boutique investment bank based out of New York. But she did recognize the name of the main contact of the client. No, it couldn't be. Too ironic! Too much of a coincidence! Were her recent thoughts about Danny some sort of premonition? Her heart beat, faster and faster.

For the remainder of the weekend, she mulled how she would make the phone call. It had been way too long. Many years too long. She finally did make it to work, on Monday. She sat in her small office, glancing at the contact information. She grabbed a mint out of her Winnie the Pooh shaped coffee mug. Then she picked up her receiver and dialed the digits, heard a ring, and hung up. This occurred two more times. Finally, she decided to let it go through.

Her heart beat faster and faster. What could she say after so many years? How could she possibly introduce herself? How could she do it without encountering some hostility? Luck took her side today. It didn't go to voicemail. She heard a name, the very name she expected to hear. Rina could not respond.

Again, the voice called out her name. "Hello? Justine Sarkar," said Sunil's wife. Sunil, Danny's best friend.

"Justine?"

"Yes."

"Hi, this is Rina. Rina Desai."

After a brief awkward pause the voice became suddenly and unexpectedly cheerful. "Oh my God, Rina? Is that you?"

"Yes, it's me. So you remember me."

"Of course," if she was being perfunctory, Rina could not tell. "How are you? Oh my God, how have you been?"

"I'm doing ok. Living in Boston."

"Really, I'm going up there tomorrow."

"Yeah, I know. I saw your name on my company guest list."

"Oh my God, that is so funny."

"Look, are you going to be staying at the Marriott?"

"Yeah, what's up?"

"Are you going to be coming alone?"

"Yes, the kid's got the flu, so he's staying in the city with Sunil." Sunil and Justine had a kid now? Things had changed.

"Do you think we can grab some breakfast at nine?"

"Uhm, yeah, I think that's doable."

"Great, I'll meet you at the lobby and let's say ten to nine?"

"Ok, see you then?"

"Oh yeah, Justine, can you do me one more thing please?"

"Sure, what's up?"

"Can you not tell Sunil just yet that you spoke to me?"

Justine had not changed. Not one bit. Rina recognized her the instant she stepped out of the elevator. "Oh my God, hi." They kissed each other on the cheek and hugged.

"Wow," Rina said. "You look amazing."

"So do you."

They decided to get breakfast at the diner across the street.

"So, how old is your boy?"

"Almost two. Are you married?"

Rina swallowed her hash brown and took a sip of her orange juice. "Yeah. But not for much longer. I filed for divorce last week."

"Aw! I'm sorry. What happened?"

"A marriage that never should've happened. That's what happened."

"Was it arranged?" It really didn't feel like Justine asked a question. Or rather she asked a question which she already had the answer too.

"Sort of." When she saw Justine staring at her incredulously, she said, "More like a forced marriage. My parents set me up with him after finding his profile on this Indian matchmaking site. I should've told them at the start that he wasn't my type. But they kept pressing and pressing when I told them that he seemed nice."

"So, was he like abusive?"

"Not physically. But it's just that he and his family have this complex about being Indian. Like his Mom has other Indians call her Mrs. Pathak, because it's too un-American for other Indians to call her Didi. He gets embarrassed if I wear Indian clothes. And oh my God you won't believe this. They even tried to get me to eat meat once. Like being vegetarian was something silly."

"Sounds like a real bunch of winners."

"You don't know the half of it," Rina went on. "Can you believe that at the wedding his father spit the rice out of his mouth because he found out the cook was Muslim!"

"Oh my God," Justine sounded genuinely disgusted, like she was watching one of the darker episodes of Law & Order SVU. "Did they just migrate over from some backward village?"

"No," said Rina. They've been here for like over thirty ears."

"Do you remember Dr. Majumdar?" Justine said.

"I don't think so, who's that?"

"I'm pretty sure you've seen them at Sunil's parents' place. She's a doctor from Queens. Her older son is dating this model."

"Oh, I think so. Is she the one who told off her priest because he was making fun of her husband for not being Brahmin?"

"Yeah," Justine laughed. "I heard what someone did at her house and she flipped out and told the person off for doing that."

"That's the way it should be."

"Yeah," Justine said. "I didn't think you'd ever get down with people who do that bullshit."

"Like I said," Rina sighed. "It's a marriage that never should've happened."

"Well, at least there are no kids involved," Justine tried to soothe her, but immediately regretted saying it, fearing being presumptuous. "There wasn't, was there?"

Rina shook her head. "No. No little Archies for me."

Justine gently put down her fork and wiped her mouth with her napkin. For the first time today, she seemed to have some sort of inimical vibes toward Rina. Justine glared at her, before finally saying, "I kind of figured that this was going to lead to Danny."

The waitress came by, a young Korean girl who couldn't have been more than twenty or twenty-one. Maybe, Rina thought to herself, that she could be a college undergrad, involved in an interracial relationship. "Would there be anything else?"

"Give us a dessert menu?" Rina said.

"Sure, no problem."

Rina looked back at Justine. "Wow, how'd you figure out I was talking about him. Was it that Archie thing?"

When Justine nodded her head, Rina said, "Are you still in touch with him? How is he?"

The waitress returned with two dessert menus. Rina asked for another glass of water.

"Well, he was pretty devastated after you broke up with him."

"That makes two of us. But how is he now? What's he been up to?"

"Well," Justine sighed. "If you really want to know. I think he's been a manager at a family restaurant for the past few years or so."

"A restaurant manager?" Rina asked bewildered. "What about that software company in Redbank?"

Justine shrugged her shoulders. "I guess they had their issues during the bust. He started busting tables for a little while and I guess he just stuck it out in the food business."

"Is he still living at home?"

"Actually, his parents retired and moved down to Charlottesville."

"Whoa, Charlottesville? You mean Charlottesville as in Charlottesville Virginia?"

"That's the one."

"Does that mean he has the house all to himself?"

"Actually they sold the house. Danny's got a place in Jersey City now."

Rina took a sip of her water. "Is he married or engaged or anything like that?"

"I think he might be seeing this Catholic School teacher."

Rina felt the cold air brush in when a customer exited the room. It reminded about the night when Danny first kissed her. It was a windy Sunday and his warm lips blanketed her. He kissed her right before he told her that he was going to raise his standards in the woman he would date. "Look Justine," Rina said. "I'm only in Boston for a few more weeks. I put in my notice at work and am going to be crashing at my parents' house in New Jersey for a bit while I figure out next steps about my life."

"Ok?"

"We used to be good friend Justine. I know I made some mistakes but . . ."

"Rina. Is there something you want from me?"

"Yes."

Danny lifted up his whole cards, peeking at his Ace of spades and four of hearts. He was on in the big blind, and Robbie, the Wall Street trader just raised the pot at the cutoff by three bets, making it fifteen dollars to go. Taking a sip of his Heineken, he glanced at this leading chip stack. "Fine, I'm curious," Danny took two red chips off his towering stack and threw them into the center of the poker table.

"Don't splash the pot," said Robbie.

"I'll splash it if I want to. What the fuck are you gonna do about it?"

"Yo man," Robbie said. "That Teddy KGB line only works when you're the host. Chill with the drinking."

Four more people called. When a rainbow flop came down including a two of clubs, three of hearts, and a five of spades, Danny touched the felt consecutively with each of the fingers of his right hand. "Thirty to go," he called out after the small blind checked. Everyone else folded with the exception of two other players, including Robbie.

The doorbell rang. "It's open," Robbie called out, and in walked Sunil Sarkar.

Sunil walked in, taking off his Banana Republic coat, and pulled up a chair right behind Danny. "Sorry I'm late fellas. Got caught up with something at work at the last minute."

"No sweat man," Danny shouted out. This game'll be over soon enough."

"You think so," said Robbie.

"Yeah."

"Ok, let's see the turn."

The dealer dealt the five of clubs. Someone's probably drawing a flush, Danny thought to himself. If they had the Ace of clubs, his chip stack would be in trouble. Can't let them catch that flush on the river. "I'm all in" Danny pushed his chips into the stack. One person immediately folded whereas Robbie without hesitation said, "Call!"

The river card came down with an insignificant seven of diamonds. "Straight!" Danny got up turning his whole cards face up. "Beat that!"

Robbie stared at him with the same expression he had throughout the game. "You're right Danny. The game's over." He turned over his own whole cards, a pair of fives. "For you. I got Quads."

"Fuck!" Danny screamed out. "Fuck me!"

Danny got up and paced around the living room. He grabbed his fleece and headed out the door. He made his way outside and took the elevator down to the streets. "Yo, Danny," Sunil rushed after him. "Dude, are you drunk man?"

"Yeah, pretty much. Fuck, I just lost my entire fucking roll on that hand. I fucking had the straight. I should've gone all in on the flop. He would've folded his set."

"Dude, you always said, that if you're gonna lose in cards, you're gonna lose with good cards, not bad ones."

"I said that to people who were losing."

"Did you drive here?"

"Nah, walked it."

"Good," Sunil smiled. "Then I don't have to wrestle you for your car keys. Can't go home to the wife and kid with a black eye."

The two childhood friends walked down four blocks until they got to Danny's building.

Danny stumbled opening the door to his place and let himself fall onto his armchair. He flipped on the television to YES network which was airing a repeat of a

Yankee and Red Sox game. Sunil made himself comfortable on the couch. "How's Joanne?"

Danny stared at him bewildered. Raising an eyebrow, he said, "Joanne?"

"Are you kidding me Mahoney? You brought her into the city like two weeks ago."

"Oh her," Danny laughed. "That waitress from Cheeseburger in Paradise. Oh, she annoyed me, so I dumped her."

"You dumped her?"

"Yeah man."

"Weren't you with her for like two weeks! I thought you said you really liked her."

Danny shrugged his shoulders. "Hey! What do I know about women?"

"Look, man, we've been best friends forever."

"Like E and Vince."

"Right, like E and Vince. But look. Even though I knew you since we were like sperm, I just can't picture what your type is. Believe me, if I knew I'd help you find her."

"My type," Danny laughed. "My type is a girl who can stand up to her family." He got up from his armchair and walked over to the dartboard resting on the far wall. Grabbing the darts, he headed over to the window where he glanced down at the courtyard.

"Come on man," Sunil said. "How many times are we gonna go through this over?"

"Dunno my friend. I just don't fucking know."

"What's it been? Like seven years? Don't you think it's time to move on! You gotta stop having these relapses about her."

Danny said nothing. He just stared into the courtyard. He saw a young Indian couple, he knew vaguely, who'd just graduated from University of Pennsylvania, walking hand in hand together into their wing of the building. The guy, Khuram, was a first year medical student at UMDNJ Newark, and he came to this complex frequently to visit his fiancé Sahar, a tech analyst at a Wall Street firm. He caught a glance of Khuram kissing the top of Sahar's head as they disappeared behind the revolving door. "Easy for you to say bro," Danny turns around to face Sunil. "Look at you now. Married to your college sweetheart. You got a kid. Look it feels like you're Ray Barone with the perfect family life and all and I'm his older loser brother who just can't get a break."

"Nah," Sunil laughed. "You're not tall enough to be Robert."

"Look, seriously. Look, you and Justine are like the perfect couple."

"No, perfect we're not. We've got our fair share of problems.

"Yeah, but you're still together. You don't let one little problem break you apart."

Sunil lifted himself up from the couch and made his way next to Danny. "Yeah man, I guess you're right. I'm sorry. I guess if Rina had more of a spine, things would've been better for you now?"

"Maybe. It's just that . . . I just can't believe she'd throw it all away . . . over what her parents might've thought . . . I mean, I don't think I'd be this bummed if we had the right type of closure, you know what I mean?"

"I hear ya. Look I'll tell you what. Friday night. Let's watch the Yankee game at Mickey Mantle's."

"Mickey Mantle's?" Danny laughed. "If you're gonna ask me to go to the city for a game, you could say 'let's go to the stadium'."

"C'mon man, it'll be fun! Like the old times. What do you say?"

Danny turned to him. "Fine. I'll be there."

The train into Penn Station was infested with people wearing Yankee caps and jerseys. Little kids were waiving their banners like the Yankees had already beaten the Mariners. Maybe it would've been better to meet up at the stadium. Someone took a seat next to her. It had been years since she commuted on the NJ Transit. Before business school took her away from the tri-state to Red Sox territory. The train stopped at Newark, and by force of habit, Rina got up to leave and transition to the path train when it occurred to her that she was not going to downtown New York. Not this time. At Penn Station, she joined the long line riding the escalator and when she finally got to the street level, she found some breathing room. Everyone else was heading towards the one and two trains while she quickly made her way to the E train.

She caught a glimpse of the posters. Laura Osnes radiated her beauty in the picture that she was promoting for her Broadway show Grease. The first Broadway show she saw was Aida. She saw it with Danny the autumn after she graduated from college. She missed New York. Everything here was so centralized, a subway ride away. Getting off at 42nd Street to switch to the R train, Rina sat herself down as the subway took off, taking her pocket mirror out of her purse. She stared at herself.

"Don't sweat it Honey, you look gorgeous!" Rina looked up to glance at a larger black woman sitting across from her, armed with a laundry cart.

"Oh, thanks," Rina smiled back at her.

"Are you off to a date?"

"No. I mean sort of."

"Sort of?" said the woman. "It's either a date or it's not. So what is it?"

"Well, I'm sort of meeting up with my ex-boyfriend."

"So it is a date."

"More like a surprise," Rina laughed. "I know we're meeting up. He doesn't."

"My my," said the woman. "How long has it been?"

"Seven years."

"Seven years? Wow. He couldn't have been all that bright for letting you go Gorgeous."

"He didn't let me go," Rina's smile slowly faded. "I was the one who wasn't all that bright."

The train reached the Central Park stop. "Well, this is my stop. It was nice talking to you."

"Honey, don't let him go this time."

"Ha," Rina laughed. "I need to get him back first."

"Honey. Listen to me. Do not let him go this time."

Rina climbed up the stairs to see a family boarding a horse carriage. "Hey senorita," called out a street artist, who looked Chinese or Korean. "How about a nice sketch?"

Instead of saying "No thanks", Rina abruptly said "How much?"

"Only fifteen dollars."

"No thanks."

"Fine, ten dollars."

Rina said nothing, but glanced to her right to see Columbus Circle and the Time Warner mall. At first she thought she saw Chelsea Clinton dressed in running shorts and a Columbia long sleeve t-shirt run past the horse carriage into the park, but she realized it was just someone who would come in maybe at most fourth or fifth in a look alike contest. Rina finally caught a glimpse of Mickey Mantle's across the street, and made her way across 59th Street. She glanced through the window. There he was, Danny Mahoney, sitting at the bar, wearing his trademark authentic Yankee cap. She still had a picture of their time at the beach together, where he was shirtless, wearing that hat backwards. He was chewing on some celery sticks and dipping his mozzarella sticks into the sauce, glancing up at the television screen.

She glanced at her reflection through the window. Taking a deep breath, she wondered what results her soon encounter would yield. She opened the door, stepped into the restaurant, ready to once again accept and be accepted.

-For Kimberly Fisher
11.14.2008

Never Over

*"Thou grieve where no grief should be," God in
the guise of the dandy Krishna tells his cousin, the
archer Arjuna. "The soul lives forever. Fire cannot
burn it, water cannot dampen it. Just as how you
discard your old clothes, and replace them with new
ones, so does the soul leave one body and enter another.
So how do you grieve for the dead when they continue
living?"* Deep knows that roughly translated, that's
what the priest, Swapan Chakravarty, recites in the
obscure Sanskrit from the Bhagavad-Gita. His mother,
Suparna, used to teach stories from the Ramayan and
Mahabharat to him and a bunch of other Bengali kids
who'd come from all the boroughs, parts of Connecticut,
Westchester, and Long Island to attend Bengali school
on Sundays. Initially, the class sessions occurred in the
basement of a family friend who volunteered their
basement of their Flushing home, but as more kids
enrolled, it became necessary to rent a room in the
basement of Northern Boulevard's YMCA. He
remembers that YMCA well, as he learned how to swim
and play basketball there, and would later have his Cub
Scouts meetings there. It is also a half-mile south from
where he is today.

"Don't cry Ma," he wants to say, but realizes
that not she but several others need consoling. Familiar
faces swarm in, many of who hold flowers. All of them
wear the visages of sadness today. He begins to wonder
when so many Bengalis from the New York area
assembled together last? Perhaps the wedding of Sunil
Sarkar to his college girlfriend Justine! Or the marriage
of Sunil's sister even before that! Maybe at a Bengali
conference! He is not sure, but he sees too many
familiar faces making their way in.

As can be expected, Chhoto and Rana come
together with their moms. As always, they stick
together, like brothers. Come to think of it, Deep's first
memory of this Genovese Funeral Parlor is back in the

early nineties, when Chhoto's father passed away from cancer. Around that time, Chhoto had stopped coming to Bengali classes on Sundays, as he was too busy cutting school, vandalizing the neighborhood, and running from the police. Deep has fond memories of growing up with Chhoto, and especially remembers him being a great basketball player and a fantastic artist. The latter attribute he demonstrated quite well with his graffiti work on public buildings and subway walls. After Chhoto constantly started to get in trouble with the police, Deep didn't really associate with him much. But he was glad to learn that Chhoto straightened out. He approaches Chhoto, and pats him on the shoulder. "Thanks for coming Chhoto, it means a lot to me." Back then, most other parents told their kids to stray away from Chhoto, citing him to be a bad influence, heading towards a criminal life. But no, Deep knew Chhoto would bounce back. Before graduating from NYU, Chhoto spent time at a junior college at Westchester where he demonstrated that his dismal high school grades didn't paint a flattering picture of how smart he really was. Chhoto now works as a successful comic book artist, with his own book and does personal portraits for many wealthy and famous people.

And Chhoto never lets anyone forget that Rana helped him through his darkest hours. "Hey Rana," he then briefly places his hand on Rana's shoulder. Rana, being six years older to Chhoto, served as both his surrogate big brother and father figure. Rana himself, lost his father, but not to death. His father walked out on the family for another woman, when Rana was but a boy. Rana became the man of his house early, and supported his mother and did the best to make her feel happy by being both a model student and son. He took odd jobs, which included being a paperboy, a pizza delivery boy, and apart time construction worker to support his mother. He would hand over his entire paycheck to his mother after each payday. Rana became the boy that all the Bengali parents wanted their sons to be like, and their daughters to marry. He certainly did not deserve a philandering wife. Only an evil woman could ever consider cheating on a man so selfless. "Chhoto was always right about you. If there's someone that we can always depend on, it's you." Rana carries two bouquets of flowers and goes straight over to the casket and lays them next to him. Chhoto follows behind him, dutifully, and both go over to hug and console the crying women.

"Hey Gopal," Deep sees the short but larger than life Bengali protégé walk in, holding his violin. "I think your brother and his wife Lisa are already here. Can't believe how big their daughter is now." Gopal smiles weakly, but sadly. For some reason, in spite of their parents being friends, he and Gopal were not particularly close growing up. Maybe it was because of their four-year age gap. He could understand why Gopal would feel morose coming here. In fact, in this very place they cremated Gopal's mother when Gopal was a senior at Swarthmore, and Deep himself was a senior at Townsend Harris High School. What a terrible time it must've been to lose a parent. "Hey Gopal," he hears the voice of his mother's childhood friend, Bhakti Majumdar say in her native Bengali. "It's nice of you to come."

Gopal goes over to give Bhakti Majumdar a hug, replying in Bengali, "It was nothing at all. How are you Mashi?"

"I've been better. I don't particularly enjoy coming here."

"I know," says Gopal. "But this is part of life."

"Yes, but not so . . ."

He interrupts her, but not rudely, when a beautiful woman, with dirty blonde hair walks in, running her fingers through Gopal's hair. Could this be Gopal's girlfriend? Deep stares at the most fascinating woman he's seen, sporting a svelte figure with perfectly shaped breasts. She places her SAAB car keys into her

NorthFace jacket pocket. She stands a head taller than Gopal. "Mashi, do you remember Melissa?"

"Of course," Bhakti Majumdar goes over to give Melissa a hug. Like Danny Tanner of Full House, she should call herself a lean mean hugging machine. "Gopal tells me you've been quite nice to him since his Mother . . ." She bursts into tears. "Life is so unfair. Gopal's mom must be so happy looking down at you, knowing how much love you've given to her son. You're a wonderful person Melissa."

"It's nothing," Melissa says. "Gopal's like a little brother to me. I'll do anything for him. Now that he quit smoking." She gives Gopal a playful elbow.

"I'm going to get this started" Gopal points to his violin case and heads over towards the casket.

Little brother? What kind of relationship do they have? He really does not know Gopal all that well he figures, but he does know that he still plays a great violin. A beautiful raga emerges from the strings of his violin.

"*I reside in the hearts of all beings, I am bigger than the biggest, smaller than the smallest, all things are part of me, I not part of them.*" Swapan Chakravarty continues to recite verses from the Gita. He is seated near the center of the casket, sitting Indian style on the ground. Next to him sits his mother, who has now been joined with Bhakti Majumdar, wrapping her arm around her. Both sob uncontrollably. "*The Soul does not die, the wise know this and does not mourn.*" If according to the Gita the wise understand immortality, then why do these two devout Hindu women mourn for the dead?

Growing up, his Mom wants him to become a gentleman. His Dad wants him to become a Doctor. Neither wants him to become a lawyer, yet that's what he precisely chooses to become after he completes studying economics and psychology. To the dismay of his father, he chooses to enroll at NYU law school. But in his heart of hearts, prior to doing anything in life, he longs to represent the United States in the Olympics. He really wants to be the first person of Indian origin to win a Gold Medal in wrestling.

In seventh grade he tries wrestling for the first time, after he gets cut from the junior high basketball team. A friend from New Jersey recommends he do this. On day one the practice kills him, and he can barely stand up straight. Limping down the hallways, he sees his mom waiting for him in the parking lot. She stands in front of their Ford Station wagon.

"I'm done," he tells her, getting into the passenger seat, and putting on his seatbelt. He ejects the tape deck that plays a Bengali song, and tunes the radio until he hears rap music. "I'm quitting wrestling. It's too tough."

"No, stick with it."

This surprises him. Normally his mother lets him do as he pleases, but she insists that he sticks with wrestling. He grows to appreciate this as wrestling not only makes him a champion, and helps him find something he's good at. It also teaches him about self-control. He wrestles varsity for four years in the middleweight division, and gets aggressively recruited by many division one schools. He chooses the University of Virginia. He wants to go the Olympics. His Dad wants him to take his MCATS.

One day he and a fraternity brother want to play a prank on a sorority. They intend to install a web cam on the window to the main bedroom. So one night, Deep and his fraternity brother Chris take the necessary equipment and head over to the sorority house. Deep climbs over the ledge of the front door. "Toss me the blanket," he says to Chris upon reaching the top.

Chris tosses it but it's out of reach. He tries to grab it anyway, but he loses balance and falls to the ground, his right knee hitting the cement. His wrestling career comes to an end, as do his hopes of going to the Olympics. His Dad insists that he studies for the

MCATs, but he chooses the LSATs. If he can't pursue a career as an athlete, then he will represent them.

But prior to attending school again for another three years, he wants to try something different. So he enrolls in Teach for America and teaches social studies at a Baltimore public school for a year. He thoroughly enjoys giving history lessons. But coaching the kids after school in track and wrestling really inspires him more. He enjoys sports. Why would he want to leave this world?

After a year, he gets accepted to NYU Law school, and also takes a job as an assistant wrestling coach at a prestigious prep school located in Manhattan's Greenwich Village. His Mother applauds his decision; his Father still voices his preference for medical school. Both are happy to have him back in New York. He too is happy. He enjoyed life closer to the Mason Dixie line, but he enjoys his hometown much more. All the friends he grew up with are here, and he gets to visit his parents much more frequently.

One night he's at Union Square, watching the college kids skateboard, doing ollies off of the staircases. He wonders if any of them are athletes. They should be careful. Life isn't fair. He could've made the Olympics. He knows it. Everyone deserves a second chance. Why can't he get another shot at the Olympics?

"Ahhh!" He sees a little girl in the middle of the road on 15th street. A speeding car is coming towards her. He rushes towards her. If he can make it on time he can grab her. He makes it just in time to push her away from the car.

"Those who seek me, at the hour of death, shall find me. Otherwise, they go on to find what they're seeking, in a new body. Always keep focused on me, be free from passions, free from addiction, and focus on me, and you'll find me at your hour of death." Swapan Chakravarty continues reciting stanzas from the Gita.

126

The funeral parlor is full and people are still swarming in. Why, he thinks to himself, wasn't he given the chance to reconcile his career choice with his father? He didn't want to have anything to do with the life sciences. And his father, a former Honors student in Chemistry at Kolkata's Presidency College, and then earned a doctorate at Stony Brook, wanted his son to share his passion. But alas, passion needs to be cultivated, not enforced. But differences can be mediated. Why, he thinks in this funeral parlor, was he denied this chance to reconcile with his father?

In walk Sunil Sarkar and his wife Justine, the latter holding their son who must be four- year old by now. He smiles. Like Gopal, Sunil is four years older to Deep, but they clicked more. Along with his parents, Deep would often travel to New Jersey to visit Sunil's family, and often would spend the entire weekend there.

Whoa, not only is Sunil here, but his friend Danny Mahoney is here too. Yes, he remembers Danny well too. Danny too would often spend the nights with them, and the three of them would camp out together in the family room, watching a horror movie until three in the morning. Danny too wrestled, and when Sunil would fall asleep, he and Danny would turn on a WWF video and watch Hulk Hogan pulverize Rody Piper. Yes, he liked Danny a lot and always wanted to hang out with him when he went to New Jersey. Danny holds hands with this Indian girl, obviously pregnant. Danny and the Indian girl follow Sunil to his mother Suparna.

Danny immediately hands his mother a white flower followed by a long hug. "Mrs. Pal. I'm really sorry. I really don't know what to say."

"Oh Danny," Deep's mother sobs inconsolably. "Why? Why did this happen to me? What did I do in my previous life to deserve this? Was I that bad a person?"

"Don't say that," Danny whispers, still hugging his mother. "Everyone knows you can't be a bad person.

A bad person couldn't have brought up a good kid like Deep."

Deep stares at his mother hugging Danny Mahoney, and finally realizes that all the people here came to attend his funeral. He indeed did save that girl from being hit by the car on 15th street, yet, he did not manage to save himself. He stares at his body deprived of its soul in the casket. Danny, still hugging his mother tightly shifts his direction towards his father who is making his way towards him. "Mr. Pal."

"Danny," Deep's father says to him. "Deep idolized you. He wanted to be just like you."

"I don't know about all that," Danny gives a sad laugh.

"No, it's true. When we'd go to Sunil's house he'd look forward most to seeing you."

"Yeah?"

"Oh yes. You're all he talked about. He wanted to be just like you. Get all those trophies and his picture in the paper. Just like you. He wrestled because that's what you did."

"Oh yeah? I thought he wrestled because he couldn't play basketball."

"That's what he might've said," his father places his hand on Danny's shoulder. "But really, he wanted to be just like you. You were the older brother he never had."

Like in a movie, the setting abruptly changes. His mother, father, Danny, and the others all disappear. It is black, Deep's floating in midair like Superman. An old man with a long grey beard and hair, clad in deerskin appears before him out of a thick filament of light, accompanied by six identically looking men. "Is this the afterlife?" Deep asks them. "My grandmother in India used to tell me stories that Indra the King of Devas, would greet people right before they'd go to Heaven."

"We appear before you the way we do because of your preconceived notions." The old man in the middle speaks with an American accent. It reminds him of his history teacher from tenth grade.

"So you're telling me if I was Christian, I'd be seeing Saint Peter?"

"Perhaps," says the old man in the middle. "Such things don't matter now."

"So how does this work? Do I get my wings now or something like that?"

The old man shakes his head. "No, not today. Not yet."

"So what, you send me to a Judgment hall? Like I get my Gold Medal?"

"No, the decision has already been made. You cannot cross us. There is no place for you here in Heaven. Not yet that is!"

"Huh? Why not? I don't think I was that bad a person."

"It doesn't matter. Your thoughts still dwell on earthly matters."

"What're you talking about? I want to see the light. I want to go there."

"If that truly was the case, we'd let you in without a moment's hesitation. Yet in your heart of hearts, you do not yet desire to become one with God," the old man in the middle shakes his head. "You're still focused on earthly achievements which you missed. You sought that at the time of your departure. That's what you will get."

"But that place is paradise. I want to go there."

"Then in your next life stay focused on the highest bliss," advises the old man. "Yet we will not let your pleas go completely in vain. As you left your previous life doing a noble deed, we will take pity on you. We assure your next life will be rewarding and long. You'll find what you seek."

"No, no! I want the light. I want to go there. Where the light is. Now."

"Sorry, we cannot offer you that right now, because you do not seek it." The seven men and the light move away from him rapidly at lightning speed.

"Hey wait," Deep tries to run towards them, but he cannot, and all of a sudden he finds himself back in Flushing, staring at his mother hugging Danny.

After several more minutes of crying and hugging, Danny introduces his parents to the Indian girl who came with him. "Mr. Pal, Mrs. Pal, this is Rina."

Rina gives both his parents a hug and then touches both their feet in deference.

"You found yourself an Indian wife?" Deep sees his father laugh sadly to Danny. "Deep would've been so amused. Remember how he used to tease you about being Indian, Danny?"

"Of course," says Danny.

"So you're married?"

"No. Not yet," says Danny, touching Rina's belly. "Not until after the baby is born."

"I'm so sorry," Rina says. "Both Danny and Sunil told me such great things about your son. I would've loved to have known him. Sounds like a wonderful person."

"Yes he was," sobs his mother. "What he really wanted to do was wrestle in the Olympics."

Rina smiles sadly and points to her belly. "Danny wants the same thing for our baby."

Deep's mother returns the sad smile. "I'm glad you're expecting. Do you know what it'll be?"

"It's a boy," Danny whispers.

"Can you believe," says Rina, "that he already has the baby on a waiting list for this wrestling camp."

"I wish it a splendid and long life," Deep's mother says. "Promise me that you'll bring him to see me."

The soul doesn't die, it attains what it seeks. Swapan Chakravarty continues to chant from the Gita.

Deep searches for the light and the seven old men, but both are light years away. He tries in vain to move towards the light, but fails. He begins to lose his memories of his life. A force, stronger than gravity, and faster than light, grabs him. He cannot break loose try as he may. Deep rapidly feels his spirit heading towards where Rina is standing.

Rina suddenly places both her hands on top of her belly. "I think my water just broke."

The Beginning . . .

- For Joydeep Sarkar (1980-2010)
01.15.2011

A special thanks to all those who've given generous feedback and support, and who had faith in me always, no matter what:

Neil Ghoshal, Joel Kraf, Gerry Wilson, De' Jon Welcome (the Proof to my Eminem), Tim Ferriss, Anirban Jana, Nabanita Biswas, Tadvana Narayanan, Chris Burke, Mike Novak, Brian Jo, Miral Sattar, Alison Waldman, Bijon Mehta, Kaiser Wahab, Amish Jhaveri, Elizabeth Cincotta, Garud Iyengar, Rakhi Datta, Payal Gandhi, Aaron Brown, Rachel Hip-Flores, Robert Barton, Krishna Lewis aka Ali Di, my preschool teacher the late Lakshmi Sarkar, Patricia Manfredi, Kanak Datta